"It's as if Douglas Adams wrote an episode of South Park while under the influence of psychotics."
- Anonymous

"By far my favorite short story series on the internet."
- Bryn

"Duuude . . ."
- Anonymous

"Such incredible stories! I read them all in one night, without putting down my phone!"
- Natasha

"The Jim stories are an adult form of a Calvin and Hobbes comic. They all espouse a kind of thought, a thought that isn't pushed on you. You're free to think about it, or just enjoy the absurdity at face value."
- /u/kawarazu

Also by Adam Spielman

Jarmo

Book of Jim

Agnostic Parables
and
Dick Jokes
from
Lucifer's Paradise

Adam Spielman

Cover and illustrations by
PAT JENSEN

Book of Jim: Agnostic Parables and Dick Jokes from Lucifer's Paradise, is a work of fiction. Names, places, and characters are products of the author's imagination or are used fictitiously. The author admits that he has neither seen Paradise nor spoken with the dead celebrities that inhabit it, and furthermore confesses that the place probably doesn't even exist and the *Book of Jim* is a lie.

ISBN: 1508895279
ISBN: 978-1508895275

www.drowningdream.wordpress.com/jim

for my parents –
who made me

and thanks to:

fangso and haines and dan and jon,

creators of the most epic fifteen minutes of film
ever produced

the /r/writingprompts community on reddit,

for the endless entertainment, ideas, and the
occasional upvote

whoever the hell *you* are (yes – *YOU*)

because you're here – and you could be reading
Gaiman or getting laid

"If you want to make an apple pie from scratch, you must first invent the universe."

– Carl Sagan

I

1

Jim ate the pizza, and it was good. There was pepperoni on the pizza, and sausage, and there were also bits of bacon. There weren't any green olives. The cheese was greasy, the crust was thick, and the sauce *was* red.

He turned and beheld the angel.

"So I'm really dead," he said.

"You're really dead," the angel said.

Jim chewed the pizza. There was also beer and he drank from the bottle and washed the pizza from his mouth with the beer.

"That's good beer."

"It's the best beer."

He looked at the image of his body upon the road, the last angle of his limbs. He thought about the darkness in the sky and its weight against his open eyes.

"So, am I a soul?" he said.

"Sure," the angel said.

"Sure?"

"Sure, you're a soul. Why do I care what you call it?"

Jim chewed some more pizza and drank some more beer, for the beer and the pizza *were* good. He beheld the angel once more. It was a shiny angel, white with wings and a halo and the halo was gold.

"I don't even believe in angels," Jim said.

"Fuck you," the angel said.

Jim opened his mouth to speak, and then he closed it. He did this *three* times.

"Well, what I meant was, I didn't used to. Believe in angels."

"Fuck you, too."

"What?"

"Fuck who you *are*, and fuck who you *were*. I don't see any difference."

The road was empty and death came easy. The angel had come out of the trees by the road and touched him on the shoulder. The touch had not been gentle. Nor had it been unkind. It was the firm hand of eternity.

"So what happens now?"

"You have to finish the pizza. And the beer. And then I will take you to *paradise*."

"I got into Paradise?"

The angel touched him again with the firm hand of eternity.

"So your life was pointless. And pathetic. Don't worry about it. *Paradise* is kind of awesome."

Jim finished the pizza and the beer and the angel ascended and Jim followed.

2

The table was laid out with all the things that Jim loved. There were chicken wings, club sandwiches, little wieners wrapped in bacon, chili fries, and the nachos *were* deluxe. There was also whiskey and beer.

Above the table there was a swing upon which a woman swung. And she was a beautiful woman,

10

naked and smiling. Jim looked upon her and ate.

"She's beautiful," Jim said.

"Her name is Cherry," the angel said. "She's been welcoming guests for many years. You're lucky. She's brilliant."

Cherry blew Jim a kiss. The kiss hovered for a moment, and it fluttered *like* a butterfly, and it sparkled *like* a fairy; then it *was* a hawk and it dove at the bulge in Jim's pants.

He *coughed*. He poured himself another glass of whiskey.

"Is Paradise really – well, you know, *paradise*?"

"That's a stupid question. Ask it better."

"I mean, I never figured this place existed at all. But I figured if it did exist, it would be pretty uptight. Like, harps and praying and shit like that. Nothing like this."

"Yes."

"What?"

"The answer to your stupid question is yes."

"Oh."

Jim ate from the table and drank from his glass and he looked upon Cherry. He thought again about death and how quick death had come. He thought about Cherry's pussy. He thought about how painful life had been.

"There must be a catch," he said.

"The only catch is that there are no catches," the angel said. "The boss doesn't care for rules. Everybody gets in, and everybody gets what they want."

"The boss?"

"Lucy. I suppose you know her as Lucifer, but he's

Lucy now. I mean, *she's* Lucy. We're all a little confused."

"Lucifer?! I thought this was Paradise!"

"It is."

And Jim drank some more, for the whiskey *was* good.

3

The angel sighed the sigh of eternity and then spoke.

"For a long time, Paradise was much like you imagined it. Harps and praying and shit. It was a peaceful, homogenous, boring little kingdom. No one danced, and no one cried.

"And no one hated not dancing and not crying more than Lucifer. He was still Lucifer then. He rose up and confronted God about how boring everything was, and sides were chosen and we fought a war.

"God never stood a chance. Angels are legion and only nine stood at his side, and not a single mortal. All it took was somebody to break the silence. Lucifer whispered in the morning and before nightfall God fell like fucking brick.

"He passed through Earth as he fell. That's why you guys have all those crazy books, telling you to get down on your knees and swallow him. It was his revenge. Some he told to swallow like this, some he told to swallow like that. It was enough. Many have suffered for it.

"I suppose he imagined that all the war, and the confusion in general, would supply him with an army in Hell. He was thinking too much like God, though. Lucifer just burned all the laws, ate Sin, and he turned Paradise into – well, *paradise*.

"Not too long after that Lucifer became Lucy. She loves to dance.

"The end."

4

Jim listened to the angel's story, and when the story was finished he leaned back and whistled. For it *was* a strange story.

"But what if I believed in God?" he said. "What if I was religious? Finding all of this out – it would be horrible."

"But you're not religious," the angel said.

"But what if I was?"

"Well, let's say you were the Pope. Popes get in just like anybody else. Except I'd be wearing a suit and I wouldn't curse as much. And I'd take you on the holy tour and congratulate you on a life well lived. And you'd get to look in on Hell and pity the damned. That sort of thing. But you're not the Pope. You're Jim from Tennessee, so you get chicken wings and bitches."

"Chicken wings and bitches?"

"And beer."

"So you'd lie to the Pope? Hey, wait a minute. Are you lying to me?"

"Nope."

"So there *are* chicken wings and bitches?"

The angel smiled and guided Jim's eyes to Cherry, who blew him another kiss. Her breasts were firm and her skin was smooth. She *was* beautiful, and Jim became *hard*.

5

He pulled out. To his surprise he spilt no seed. He spilt instead a slice of cherry pie, complete with a fork and a dapple of cream. Cherry took a bite and was satisfied.

"Sorry," Cherry said. "I really love pie after sex."

"No, that was awesome," Jim said.

In life his seed had been a nuisance. It had certainly never been pie. He shook from his tip the last of the cream and lay down on his back. His hands he clasped *behind* his head.

"So, you heard the angel and me talking, right?"

"Sure."

"About Lucy and the resistance and all that?"

"Yeah."

"And the Popes, how they get to pity the damned even though nobody gets damned anymore? Except for God, I guess. Which seems pretty fucked up."

"Mmm-hm."

"Is that the same story he told you?"

"Kinda."

"What do you mean, *kinda*?"

"Well, I kinda forgot."

"What?!"

"It was a long time ago."

So Jim wrestled with his thoughts while Cherry ate the pie. He had never wrestled such thoughts before, and the experience was new. His brain made waves that his consciousness could *not* articulate. After a struggle, he spoke.

"If part of this place is hearing what you want to hear, how do you know what's what? Like, who's got the right of it? How do we know what's true?"

Cherry swallowed some pie and shook her fork.

"Oh yeah, the paradox thingy. The *catch-no-catch*. I wouldn't waste any time on it. Like, this is *paradise*, right? Everything you ever wanted. I mean, why do you care if there aren't any catches?"

"But there *is* a catch."

"Only if there *isn't* one."

"Well, yeah. I mean, that's what's bothering me. What if I want to know the Truth?"

Then Cherry held up the last morsel of pie. It shivered upon the fork. She said, "This is the fucking truth, honey." And she ate it.

6

Then the world began to shake. Jim jumped up from the bed and he was naked and afraid, yet Cherry lay sublime.

"Wow, that must really be bothering you," she said.

"What? Why? What's happening? Is it bad? It seems bad." Jim struggled for balance in the shaking world.

"Lucy's coming. She comes around sometimes, usually if your vibes are tangled. Don't worry, she's super nice. Tell her you like her dress."

There was a warbling *whoomf* and a hole came into the shaking world. From the hole came an ageless woman. She wore a summer dress and shades and she walked tall in sandals. There was a second warbling *whoomf* and the hole in the shaking world was no longer a hole, and the world ceased to shake. The ageless woman removed her shades and spoke.

"Cherry! You indigo slut, it's been ages! How are you?"

The two women hugged, one ageless and the other sublime. Jim was merely naked.

Cherry said, "This is Jim. He's vibing pretty hard about the *catch-no-catch.*"

"Jim." Lucy held out her hand. Jim didn't take it

right away, for it *was* the devil's hand. It was milk white and the nails were painted sharp. Then he shrugged and took it.

"I like your dress," he said.

Lucy laughed. Soon the three of them were laughing together. One was ageless, one was sublime, and Jim was naked.

"Well, I do hate these formalities, but there is bureaucracy even in *paradise*." Lucy pulled from her blouse a white business card. "If you ever want to know the Truth, just find the address on this card. They'll fill you in on everything."

"Really?" Jim said. "Just like that?"

He took the card. On it was written TRUTH in dark ink, and beneath TRUTH was written the address: 1 Truth Road.

"So I can just go down to 1 Truth Road any time I want and get the Truth? Why don't you just tell me now, save me the trip?"

Lucy's pout was sexual. Everything about her was ageless and sexual.

"Well, if you go to 1 Truth Road you can't come back."

"I can't come back? Like, to *paradise*? Why not?"

"I can't tell you that. It's part of the Truth."

"So the Truth is the *catch*."

"The Truth is the Truth. There are no *catches*."

Lucy rested a hand on Jim's shoulder. She put her lips upon his ear and she whispered.

"My advice is always the same. You have an eternity to enjoy yourself. The Truth can *wait*."

Then she kissed his ear, and she kissed his shoulder. She kissed his left nipple and his right nipple and then she kissed his stomach. Jim became *hard* and she took him into her mouth. And it was kind of awesome.

He spilt upon the ground a bucket of chicken wings, a side of mashed potatoes *with* gravy, heavily seasoned French fries, jalapeno poppers, and a chocolate milkshake.

When the devil departed, Cherry took up a wing from the bucket and offered it to him. He ate thereof, and then he ate the rest of it too.

II

1

Cherry said to Jim, "So you ready for a good time? I know just the place."

And Jim said, "Uh, sure."

So the two of them went to the place where the Orgy *was.* The beach lay nameless beneath the clear sky and the sand lay untouched and smooth. Above the beach and in the sky the Orgy flew. For it was a ship, and the ship was red and gold and it flapped two giant wings.

"There's only one way up," Cherry said. She pointed to a wooden catapult. It was the only *thing* on the beach.

"Aren't you coming?" Jim said.

Cherry shook her head. "I need some R'n'R. You know, watch some Ghostbusters, ride some dolphins, maybe some Thai food. That sort of thing."

"I like Thai food."

Cherry laughed. "You're sweet, Jim." She kissed him on the cheek. "Maybe *too* sweet."

Jim climbed into the wooden spoon of the catapult. "But wait," he said. "How do I get ahold of you? I mean, you know, if we wanted to get together."

"Oh! I almost forgot!" Cherry drew a smart phone from her purse and handed it to him. "I'm supposed to give this to you. All the essentials are preloaded. Google Paradise and Grandma Finder and everything. My number's in there too."

Jim said, "Cool." He put the smart phone in his pocket. "Well, uh, any advice? For the Orgy?"

"Don't freak out," she said. "Everything grows back."

She pulled the lever of the wooden catapult and the catapult went *thwump.* Jim took to the air, and he soared *through* the air and said, "Sheeeeyyaaaaaat!" Then he went through a portside window of the red-gold ship with wings that was called Orgy.

2

Jim wasn't alone in the cabin of the ship that was called Orgy. There was also a bald bespectacled man who carried kind eyes and a clipboard. And he *was* kind.

"Welcome," the bald bespectacled man said. "Is it Jim?"

"Yeah," said Jim. "How do you know my name?"

"Because you're right on time." The bald bespectacled man made a mark on his clipboard with a ball point pen. "If you'll just walk with me, we can get you sorted on the way."

"Are you another angel?"

"Nope."

They walked through a door and into a hallway and the hallway had many doors.

"So Jim, it says here that you're straight. Is that correct?"

"Uh, yes. Definitely straight."

"Would you say you're straight like an arrow, or straight by default?"

"I, um, I guess I never thought about it like that. Let's go with default."

"And do you prefer intimacy or anonymity?"

"Intimacy."

"You see three women. One is wearing black, one white, the other red. Choose one."

"White."

"Ass, mouth, or pussy?"

"What?"

"Gun to your head. Ass, mouth, or pussy?"

"Pussy."

"Great. You're doing great, Jim." The bald bespectacled man licked his fingers and flipped to the next page on the clipboard. "It says here you used to fantasize about the sixteen-year-old daughter of your uncle's neighbor. Are you still interested in young girls?"

"I, uh, I mean – sixteen?" Jim coughed, and it was a nervous cough. "Come on. She's at least, like, more than that. I wouldn't – you know. Come on. I wouldn't."

"It says here you would."

"Well, I mean, I would."

"Great. This all paints a pretty clear picture. Default hetero, preferences for intimacy and innocence and pussy, mildly suppressed desire for young girls. Not too young, I hope?"

"What? No. Man. Just give something between eighteen and forty. Keep it simple."

The bald bespectacled man murmured. It was a knowing murmur. He flipped through four pages on the clipboard, and then he clucked with his tongue.

"Well you're just in luck, Jim. Seventeen and fresh from the circus. She died about the same time you did. Blonde hair b-cup virgin, and she wants a big hairy man to savage her. Right this way."

3

The room was cozy and private. In it there was a white bed and upon the bed lay a young woman whose skin was crisp and pale. She wore white lingerie and her blonde hair was long behind her. She didn't wear make-up. The bedposts *were* mahogany.

"Hi," Jim said. "I'm Jim. I died a few days ago. Same as you, I guess."

The young woman said nothing. She wasn't beautiful, but she *was* pretty. She sucked on her bottom lip and touched herself.

Jim thought of the daughter of his uncle's neighbor and the wonderful acts he had imagined upon her. And he also thought of the daughter of his boss and the wonderful acts he had imagined upon *her*. He thought of all the wonderful acts he had imagined upon daughters, and sisters, and mothers, and he discovered that *imagining* was other than *performing*.

For she was virgin, and he was big and hairy.

He said to the virgin, "I don't want you to get me wrong, cause you're gorgeous, but I'm feeling kind of weird about this. I mean, are you sure you want to get savaged? By me?"

"Are you a lumberjack?" the virgin said.

"A lumberjack? Well, not really. I did some tree trimming for a while."

The virgin quivered, and she touched herself with *force*. "Savage me," she said.

So Jim climbed into the bed with the virgin. With his big hands he pushed her small shoulders into the mattress.

She was a terrible kisser, for her tongue was eager and unpracticed. It was therefore that he ceased to kiss her mouth and took his lips to her pussy.

And it was a terrible pussy, for it was unwashed and hairy and the odor was acrid. It was therefore that he ceased to kiss her pussy and formed with his lips a question.

"How did you die?"

The virgin said, "It doesn't matter. Please just put that lumberjack dick inside of me."

"I think I have to know."

"Fine. It was leukemia. I had leukemia for a long time and it sucked and I never got to have any fun and then I died. Now put your dick in me."

"Oh man," Jim said. "You're a kid with cancer? I don't think I should be doing this."

"Just give me your dick! I just want your big hairy lumberjack dick!"

But Jim didn't give the virgin his dick. He stood from the bed and walked to the door. "I'll have them send a real lumberjack," he said. And he went *through* the door and back into hallway of the ship that was called Orgy.

4

Jim wandered through the halls of the ship that was called Orgy for twelve days. He searched for the bald bespectacled man who carried kind eyes and a clipboard, and who *was* kind, because he wanted to make sure that the virgin received her lumberjack. But he couldn't find the bald bespectacled man, nor anybody else, and he wandered alone.

He passed by many doors, but he dared not open one. Inside there might be virgins, and he was *not* a lumberjack.

On the twelfth day he came to an elevator. In the elevator were many buttons. These are the buttons in the elevator in the hallway of the ship that was called Orgy:

Hetero-generic; Homo-generic; Bi-generic; Trans-generic; Pan-sexual; Teens and Virgins; MILFS; Anal; Submission and Domination; Legs, stockings, and feet; Traps; Gangbangs and reverse gangbangs; I just want a rim-job, bro; I'm feeling lucky.

And there was another button, *away* from the others, and the word upon it was written in flame. The word was MANIAC. Jim said, "Fuck it," and he pushed the MANIAC button.

5

So Jim came to the Pleasure Dome. The dome was high and the space was wide, and he beheld within it the orgy of the flesh of wild souls.

There *was* a bulletin board, and upon it were posted several upcoming challenges and events. There was a kick-fucking endurance challenge, an under-vodka deepthroat relay, a long distance ejaculation competition, and an aerial Kama Sutra exposition.

Jim went to the bar. He ordered a neat whiskey. A woman approached him. Her curves were thick and her swagger *was* supernal. She drank a martini.

"You must be new," she said.

"How did you guess?"

"You look confused. But mostly it's the way you're not fucking anybody right now."

"Anything I should know about this place?"

"Well, there aren't any hard rules, but raping is bad etiquette. I wouldn't kiss anybody, either."

This was a strange juxtaposition. "Why no kissing?"

The woman set down her martini and whispered into his ear, "Lips lie. Fucks fly."

So they fucked upon the bar. It was not intimate, nevertheless it was awesome. When they finished, Jim fired his ejaculate high into the dome and it was a firework that flashed and made an emerald glow.

And beneath the emerald glow Jim beheld the aerial Kama Sutra exposition. Couples launched themselves from a trampoline through the uprights of a goal post. They posed at the zenith, and their form and style were judged by card-wielding men.

He beheld a carnival ride that shot sex parties straight up into the dome, where it shook until the party climaxed, then plummeted at freefall back to the ground.

He beheld another angel, greater than the first, who stood on a platform at the center of the orgy. The angel was cut like a diamond and he had a shock of white hair. His teeth were yellow.

"Beelzebub." The woman with supernal curves took Jim's hand. "Come. Fly with me."

They came to the platform and saw that it was covered with white dust. And it was angel dust, for Beelzebub produced it by the scratching of his scalp. The *flakes* of his scalp became dust.

The angel said, "Fly like the angels fly. Feel what the angels feel. Fuck as the angels fuck."

"Okay," said Jim.

He and the woman with supernal curves snorted up the angel dust.

6

With the borrowed wings of the angel's dust Jim and the woman flew. They felt too, and fucked. And being high Jim beheld the orgy with new clarity.

He saw a thousand souls on their knees with their faces down and asses prone. Behind them stood a thousand more with oiled feet. A whistle blew, and the thousand feet kick-fucked the thousand asses, and the moans were the mingling of pain and satisfaction.

24

He saw a great mattress and upon the mattress a greater number lounged. They fucked at leisure and drank wine from goblets and they conversed about the ephemeral.

He saw the pools of vodka and the breathless race to make men cum. He saw the longest cummer crowned. The crown was made of pearls, and it was claimed by a woman who wore it *rightly* as a queen.

And Jim turned to the woman with supernal curves, who flew *beside* him, and he said, "Let's blow a hole through the dome."

So they fucked some more. It was intense fucking, and there was much grunting and ululating. As they approached the climax, Jim put his mouth upon the woman's mouth. It *was* a kiss.

The woman pulled her face away and Jim saw his mistake in her eyes.

"Lips lie," she said.

The borrowed wings molted and Jim fell.

III

1

Jim woke up on a comfortable couch. The couch was in a room and in the room there was a window. An angel sat before the window and looked out through the lens of a telescope and munched on a bowl of popcorn.

Jim knew the angel. "You're the angel that brought me here," he said.

"I am." The angel laughed at something Jim couldn't see. He popped a kernel of the popcorn into his mouth. "I heard you didn't waste any time."

"I can't hardly remember anything." Jim sat up and his head imploded. "What the hell? I have a headache."

Ca-*drum*.

"That surprises you?"

Na-*drum*.

"I thought this was *paradise*." Jim rubbed the temples of his head with the palms of his hands. He remembered the angel with the white shock and the yellow teeth and the woman with supernal curves. He remembered the kiss. "How can there be headaches in *paradise*?"

Ca-*drum* na-*drum*.

"Well," said the angel, "One way to do it is by mixing booze with angel dust."

Jim stood and stretched his limbs. He blinked four times and then he yawned and scratched himself.

The angel laughed again and munched the popcorn.

"What the hell are you laughing at?"

"The Ukraine is in revolt," the angel said. "They are wearing kitchen armor and lighting garbage on fire. Come, take a look."

Drum ca-*nun* ca-*drum*.

So Jim put his eye to the lens of the telescope. He beheld a city street at dusk. On the street a line of riot police advanced against a ragged hoard. The vestments of the hoard *were* from kitchens and closets, and the weapons of the hoard *were* from garden sheds.

The street was black with fire and the blackfire glittered over broken glass. Molotov cocktails flashed yellow when they bit into the riot shields. Many lay dead and dying. Jim saw at last a man with a noodle strainer for a helm, who was beaten into death by the batons of the police. He turned away.

Drum ca-*nun* ca-*drum* ca-*nun* ca-*drum*.

"Is that really happening? Like, on Earth?"

"Yep."

"Why is that funny?" Jim declined the angel's popcorn.

"Well in truth it isn't *that* funny," the angel said. "You should have seen Carthage. Now that was a good show. Or Nanking, or Rwanda. This revolt isn't bad for a slow decade, though."

"You watch us suffer for *entertainment*?"

Drumma ca-*drumma* na-*drumma* ca-*nun* ca-*drum*.

"Suffering is the only thing you're good at," the angel said.

"Oh come on." Jim rubbed the temples of his head with the palms of his hands. "What about baseball? We're pretty good at baseball."

"You're terrible at baseball. Angels play it with a moon and the energies of light."

"I mean, there's good stuff, too. Like, weddings and celebrations. Art and architecture. You know, the *good* stuff."

"Did *you* enjoy weddings?"

"Well, no."

Jim's head imploded some more. The pain was too much and he went to his knees.

"Fuck," he said. "Why are we so good at suffering? Why do we suffer at all?"

Drumma ca-*nun*-drum.

2

BANG!

The door burst open and through it came the bald bespectacled man, who *was* kind. Instead of a clipboard he carried with him a manila envelope.

"Jim! Well you certainly don't waste any time, do you?" And the bald bespectacled man handed the manila envelope to Jim.

Jim accepted the envelope. "Did the virgin get her lumberjack?"

"Thirty-nine of them and counting. She's got quite the appetite."

"That's good." Jim looked upon the envelope. "What is this? Why are you here?"

"It's a summons. I'm afraid you've been served. But don't worry, Jim. Just keep your chin up and everything will come out alright. Angel." The bald bespectacled man nodded at the angel and then departed.

"He tried to hook me up with a virgin. At the orgy," Jim said. "And now he's summonsing me?"

"Happens a lot around here," said the angel. "I moonlight as a jazz pianist."

So Jim opened the envelope and inside there was a single sheet of paper. He read it aloud:

Jim v Logic

You are hereby commanded to appear in the Court of Existence to defend yourself in the above-titled case and to answer to the following charge(s)

Charge(s): Asking a loaded question.

Court of Existence

Jean Paul Sartre Courthouse

Downtown, Paradise

"What the hell is a loaded question?" Jim said.

"I think it means you're full of shit," the angel said. And he put his eye to the telescope, munched on the popcorn, and laughed.

3

Jim had defended himself in court before, but that was in Tennessee and for a traffic violation. He doubted his abilities extended to loaded questions in the Court of Existence in *paradise*. So he took out his smart phone and he searched for:

"human suffering" AND "loaded question" AND "lawyer".

There was *one* result. The result was William and William: Defense Attorneys for the Anguish'd Heart. And their offices *were* in Downtown, Paradise.

So he came to a small office building nestled into one of the many corners of the city. Inside he found a single space, cluttered with parchments and books, and perched on a pile of books was the countenance of William Shakespeare.

"What's the charge?" Shakespeare didn't look up, for

he was buried in a tome.

"I, uh, I asked a loaded question," Jim said.

"The question?"

"Why is there suffering. In the world. Why do people suffer."

"Well, it would seem you've come through the right door." Shakespeare closed the tome. "Please, have a seat."

There were no chairs in the office, so Jim gathered six large books and stacked them one upon the other and he sat.

"You're William Shakespeare," he said.

"I am."

"I thought you hanged all the lawyers."

"I did." Shakespeare found a scrap of parchment and drew a pen from his shirt pocket. "A man cannot always choose how he employs his talents. But he is only lost if he doesn't employ them at all."

"Did *you* say that?"

"Yes. Just now I said that."

"Cool."

Shakespeare snapped his fingers. "The summons," he said. Jim handed him the summons and he looked upon it and sighed. "These relativisms are wearisome. What were the circumstances?"

"Well," Jim said, "I was looking through this angel's telescope, I think it was the Ukraine we were looking in on, and some really nasty stuff was going on. The angel thought it was pretty funny, which didn't really click in my head, you know? So I asked him about the suffering."

"What did you say exactly?"

"Well, let's see. I said, *Fuck. Why are we so good at*

suffering? Why do we even suffer?"

"That's it?"

"Yeah, that's it."

Shakespeare scribbled many lines across the parchment. He blotted twice, and at each blotting he frowned, pursed his lips, looked at the wall, snapped his fingers, and then he wrote something new. He finished with the flourishing of his pen.

He said, "Well, Jim, take comfort in this. It is not merely your heart, but the human heart, that is on trial. These existentialists reach too far. The question might have fallen from worthier lips, but worth is not the question."

"Great," Jim said. It sounded like good news. He stuck out his hand and Shakespeare shook it. "So you'll take the case? And you think we'll win? I mean, you're William Shakespeare, right?"

"I've yet to win a case," Shakespeare said. "But all morrows begin without sorrow, and tomorrow these hearts will beat against the narrows. Of logic. Beat against the narrow straights that constrict the mind. Hmmm." He frowned, pursed his lips, looked at the wall, then he snapped his fingers and said, "Embattled hearts are guilty when they quiver, but beating shape the world that minds arrest."

Jim was *not* a poet, and he understood only the first sentence. "Am I fucked?" he said.

"Pretty much," said Shakespeare.

4

The courtroom was a courtroom. There was a judge, a bailiff, a reporter, and there *were also* some lawyers. Jim sat with Shakespeare in the back of the courtroom. They waited for their case to be called.

The case that went before them was case twenty-two, and the lawyer who prosecuted on behalf of Logic was Immanuel Kant. He walked on stiff legs and wore a beard. It was a luscious beard, and many luscious words came out of *it*.

It was a young girl whose case was twenty-two. Jim came to understand that she had used a *slippery slope* regarding the *origins question*, and that slipping down the slope was an *assault against reason*. She was guilty before the twelfth minute passed. As punishment she received a signed copy of Kant's book about metaphysics.

"Well that doesn't seem so bad," Jim said.

"You've never read Kant," said Shakespeare.

Then the bailiff stood. "Now appearing before Judge Russell, case twenty-three, Jim v Logic."

Jim followed Shakespeare to the defendant's table. They waited for the bailiff to say more words.

"The defendant is accused of discharging a loaded question into the face of human suffering."

"Plead," Judge Russell said.

"Guiltless," Shakespeare said.

"Prosecution, go ahead."

So Immanuel Kant took the courtroom floor. He was small and arrogant and he stroked his luscious beard with his *left* hand. He said,

"The defendant, hereafter referred to as Jim, asked of an angel, Why is there suffering? This is not an innocent question. It has been sufficiently established that this line of inquiry leads nowhere, and that it debases Logic and fugues the Mind. As it is the purpose of this Court to disabuse Paradise of bad thinking, it is the Court's Imperative to hold Jim accountable for these words. The question was loaded, and he fired it like grapeshot over Prussia."

"Prussia?" Jim said.

"Objection!" Shakespeare wielded his pen. "There is no Prussia!"

"Overruled."

"Damn!"

So Kant continued. "Why is there suffering? The underlying assumption is clear. Embedded in the question is the bold assertion that the tragic nature of mortality is somehow transcendent, that it is tragic *because.* The question asserts that pain and misery have defensible, perhaps even noble, functions. It is a claim whose magnitude embroils even the most practiced Minds, and Jim offered no evidence to support it. He blithely assumed it, and he buried the assumption in six retarded syllables.

"The prosecution will happily drop the charges if Jim can defend the assumed position. If Jim can make the case for meaningful suffering, and raise the foundation necessary to support his assumption, he is free to go. If not, the prosecution is bound by the Court's Imperative to seek the maximum reprisals.

And if I may append an editorial, the presence of an angel compounds the depravity of the offense. It is disheartening that not even the wards of Paradise are safe from these stupidities."

Kant glared at Jim with his *left* eye, and he stroked his beard with his *left* hand, and then he sat down.

5

And Judge Russell said, "Can the defendant provide evidence that humankind suffers meaningfully?"

"That's *my* question," Jim said. "You're asking me the question that you're prosecuting me for asking. It's the same question."

"No," said Judge Russell. "Your question was unlettered, and it arbitrarily presupposed an ontological argument. Do you have such an argument prepared, or don't you?"

"I don't. But you guys are just being dicks. If you get to put me on trial for being stupid, I should get to put you on trial for being dicks."

"Objection. Argumentative."

"Sustained."

"What?! You're the ones that asked for a fucking argument!"

Shakespeare put a hand on Jim's shoulder. "If it pleases the Court," he said, "I'll put these quibbles to rights."

"Proceed."

So Shakespeare took the floor. He took it with classical swagger. He said,

"The Court's Imperative is the noblest undertaking in the history of humankind. Of that we have no doubt. To scour the plane of Paradise for wayward dreaming, and to smash such dreaming against the crags of progressive thinking – what pursuit could challenge it? So I salute you. Jim salutes you. Well done, gentlemen, indeed.

"And I commend the prosecution's handling of the case. A picture painted any clearer would confound the edges of the scene depicted. My client, Jim, has irrefutably asked a question to which he himself cannot apply an answer – an egregious affront to the dynasties of good thinking. I assure you that Jim has expressed to me a grave remorse, and that he is horrified at the prospect that the meat of his brain is a weight on the wings of your wonderings. But the deed was done. The question was asked.

"But is it worse to think a stupid thought, or never to have thought to think at all? The Court's Imperative may justly hold to vain account the meaty brains of men, and through its justice might preserve the meat it means to spoil. And though my client is on trial for tossing questions, I would toss the Court another:

"What soul in Paradise would shine so dull, as one by Reason painted nub to skull?"

"Objection. Poetry."

"Sustained."

"My client in his Heart defies the Pang your coward Minds pretend to understand! He asks in earnest what the prosecution merely quoths beneath bombastic veils!"

"Mr. Shakespeare, I advise you to be less poetic and more reasonable."

"The question is the food that feeds the soul!"

"Bailiff, remove the poet."

So the bailiff took Shakespeare by the shoulders and removed him from the courtroom. And Jim stood alone at the defendant's table in the Court of Existence.

6

And Judge Russell said, "The defendant, Jim, shown here to be guilty of discharging a loaded question into the face of human suffering and in the presence of an angel –"

"And over Prussia!"

"Yes, over Prussia." Judge Russell took out from his pocket a tiny cannon and placed it on the bench. "As Jim loads his questions with superfluities, the superfluities of his person shall be loaded into this tiny cannon, and fired in no particular direction."

Kant approached the bench and he handed the judge three books. The two men conferred.

"Furthermore," said Judge Russell, "Jim shall be required to read and comprehend the ontologies of Sartre, Heidegger, and Spinoza before coming aground."

The bailiff took Jim by the shoulders and dragged him across the courtroom. Jim couldn't remember a courtroom movie in which this circumstance had arisen, so he had no objection to make. Therefore his *whole person* was stuffed into the tiny canon.

Three books followed him, and they *were* the ontologies of Sartre and Heidegger and Spinoza, and each book bonked him on the head. In the circle of light at the end of the barrel of the tiny cannon, he beheld the glare of the *left* eye of Kant.

"Seriously, why are you such a dick?" he said.

And the left-eyed glare of Kant glared *lefter*. "And still he loads his questions! I move that the Court extend his sentence to include the meditations of Descartes and all the paragraphs of Aristotle!"

So two more books bonked Jim on the head, and they *were* the meditations of Descartes and the paragraphs of Aristotle.

Then there was a flick, a hiss, and a boom. Jim crashed through a window and became a bullet over *paradise*. The five books flapped about him as pigeons and they pecked at his arms and legs. Until he grabbed one and began to read:

"Modern thought has realized considerable progress by reducing the existent to the series of appearances which manifest it."

Jim thought, Well there goes eternity.

IV

1

Forty years came to pass. Jim passed over mountains and oceans and deserts. He passed over entire worlds. He passed over the plane of *paradise* until the plane was no more, and the land and the sky fell away to darkness.

And Jim was still no closer to solving existence. For though he read the ontologies *of* Sartre and Heidegger and Spinoza, and the meditations *of* Descartes, and the paragraphs *of* Aristotle, he *was* Jim.

So he remained in motion through the darkness at the edge of *paradise*. Without light by which to read, he meditated on the vague impressions of the first reading, and he made things much worse.

For he took the *cogito* of Descartes, the *bad faith* of Sartre, and the *phenomenology* of Heidegger, and he mashed them up in his brain until he became convinced that there were an infinite number of Jims. And this infinity, forever present throughout time and space, denied reality to all *particular* Jims. Therefore all Jims were also not Jim, and this *particular* Jim was here and now and then he *wasn't*. And then he *was*. And then he *wasn't*.

In this anguish and through darkness he moved.

2

It was in the fortieth year that the darkness broke. It was broken by two lights in the distance. Jim couldn't tell whether the lights moved towards him, or he towards the lights, for there was no frame of reference. But the lights got bigger and bigger, until they became the headlights of a 1969 Ford F-100 pick-up truck.

A head popped out of the driver's side window. The face was old and electric. The eyes were deep and frazzled hair jumped out of the head. Jim knew the face.

"Einstein?"

"You goddamn crazy hillbilly!" Einstein said. "I finally found it! The edge of *paradise*, I had it at my fingertips, and you blew it out your noggin!"

"Me?"

"That goddamn hillbilly brain of yours. I don't know what you've been thinking, or how you thought it up, but for the love of science forget about it. Get in, I'll explain on the way."

So Jim got in and Einstein floored it. The engine of the 1969 Ford F-100 pick-up truck roared. There was still no frame of reference but Jim could feel the acceleration of the truck, and the darkness became as a bumpy gravel road.

"What's wrong with thinking?" Jim said. He wanted there to be something wrong with his thinking, but he couldn't think of a reason for it.

"Not all thinking. Certain kinds of it. *Philosophy.*"

"So what's wrong with philosophy?"

"It's phenomenally retarded."

"What?"

"This place, *paradise*, it gives dimensionality to our thoughts. It is difficult to picture, but think of spacetime as the surface of a balloon, a very big balloon, and everything you experience is experienced on that surface. All of these fulfilled desires must occupy a certain amount of spacetime on the surface area of the balloon, and each new desire expands it. Without expansion there can be nothing new. The obvious question, then, is what fuels the expansion? What fills the balloon?"

Jim guessed, "Dark matter." Einstein ignored this and continued,

"It is our thoughts themselves, the volume of which is perfectly proportional to the surface area of the phenomenal sphere, as long as the thoughts produce phenomena. If you want a turkey sandwich, the desire fills the balloon, the sandwich occupies the surface, and proportionality is preserved. If, however, you wonder why the turkey sandwich *is* a turkey sandwich, the wonder fills the balloon but there is no surface expansion to compensate. Do you see why this is problematic?"

"Kind of."

"Soon there will be too much air in the balloon, and *paradise* will *pop*!"

Jim considered this in silence. For though Einstein had forbidden thinking, he had said nothing about *consideration*. So the 1969 Ford F-100 pick-up truck roared through the gravel of darkness, and Jim considered spacetime and phenomenal spheres. When the considering time was over, he said,

"So, what you're saying is, philosophy is bullshit."

"And it will destroy *paradise*."

"And if that's true, then there aren't really an infinite number of Jims."

"What!? Who is Jim?!"

"I'm Jim."

"You goddamn crazy hillbilly!"

3

So Jim came to the edge of *paradise*, and he beheld

that it was a brick wall. The brick wall went up forever, it went down forever, and it went to both sides forever. It *was* infinite. And at the bottom there was a neat row of hedges and a sidewalk and the sidewalk was lit with lampposts.

Einstein parked the 1969 Ford F-100 pick-up truck in the parking lot next to a public restroom. There were also some benches and swingsets and picnic tables and an Information Gazebo. On the asphalt lay a flyer that said, Live Death on the Edge! And beneath the slogan were some directions.

Jim said, "This place used to be a tourist trap?"

Einstein nodded. "The edge was once a twenty dollar cab ride. But as philosophy approaches the critical point of asininity, the expansion of *paradise* makes the journey impractical."

"So why are we here?"

"I need to go through."

"Through the brick wall?"

"To the other side. To the *antiverse*."

Einstein went forth along the sidewalk and Jim followed. Though the scientist strolled with a firm gait, Jim struggled to keep his feet, and several times he began to float away. Upon each floating, the scientist grabbed him by the foot and pulled him back into orientation.

Upon the last floating Jim began to think. He thought, If Einstein goes through the brick wall, doesn't the *antiverse* just become more *paradise*? If there's a place beyond places, and you get there, then what's beyond that? I mean, you've got to be *someplace*.

And the brick wall receded by the measure of the width of Jim's head.

"Hillbilly!"

Einstein was probably right-side-up, but Jim could not deny the sensation that he was a wonderful center, and the universe turned about him. And if he *was* a wonderful center, then Einstein was sideways and the sidewalk was a ladder.

And the brick wall receded by the measure of the width of Jim's head squared.

So Einstein grabbed him by the foot and pulled him once more into orientation. "What are you thinking? Out with it! Our proximity to the edge is intensifying its expansion. Out with it!"

"Well," said Jim, "if *paradise* expands because of thinking, and you're thinking about the *other side* of *paradise*, doesn't that mean that *paradise* includes the *other side* of *paradise*?"

"No!"

"Well why not?"

"Brick. Fucking. Wall."

Einstein pointed, and Jim once more beheld the brick wall. It *was* impressive. But not *that* impressive, he thought. If there was an *other side*, the wall could hardly be *infinite*. And what about going right or left, to the place where the wall ended? Was there more than one *other side*? Unless the wall was really a big hollow sphere and *paradise* was *inside* of it. But then, the *other side* would really be the *outside*. And what was outside of *that*?

And the brick wall receded by the measure of the width of Jim's head cubed.

Einstein shook him by the shoulders. "Listen to me very carefully," he said. "All that we can do is observe that there *is* a wall. Once the observation is made, it is our task to break *through* the wall. We must not dwell upon it, because dwelling just pushes it further away. Such is philosophy. But we are here for science, Jim. Science!"

This made some sense to Jim. He said, "So it's like, focus on what's in front of you. Start with what you can see."

"Precisely," Einstein said. "And in front of you is a wall."

So the two of them stood in silence and beheld the wall together. And when the idea came to Jim, he flinched at it, for he expected the wall to recede. The wall remained.

"What about the truck?" he said.

"The truck?"

"That thing is a classic. Last of the Mercury M series and the first with a Windsor V8. I'll bet her frame is good old-fashioned steel, too. She might get you through this wall."

"Well," said Einstein, "perhaps if I drive *really* fast."

4

Jim stood on the sidewalk at the bottom of the infinite brick wall. He watched as Einstein pulled the truck out of the parking lot and drove it far into the darkness. Jim couldn't join him, for quoth the scientist,

"You're too dumb to bring back useful information."

The truck looped around and once more Jim beheld the two lights in the distance. They grew larger and became closer at a pace that *was* beyond his comprehension. He sucked a breath, time quivered in the gaps of space, and then there was a big crash.

In the wall there was a hole in the shape of the truck. Jim thought, It's like Looney Tunes. Einstein just Looney Tuned a Ford into the *antiverse*.

But he didn't look *through* the hole, for he was afraid of what he might think about *that*, and what such thinking might destroy.

Then a plain white envelope floated through the hole. It was addressed to: Jim, Near the Hole in the Infinite Wall at the Edge of *paradise*. Jim took up the envelope and opened it, for it *was* addressed to him, and he found inside a letter and a pair of dice. The dice were glossy red. The letter said,

Dear Jim,

It worked! You goddamn crazy hillbilly, it worked! The *antiverse* is at the mercy of the powers of observation. The spacetime here is a bit outrageous though, and my observations will take a while, so don't wait up. If you have trouble finding your way back, just think of the biggest number you can think of, and then add one to it. That should do the trick.

Albert Einstein

PS

I found the dice hiding behind the wall. I have no use for them. Good luck, hillbilly!

So Jim took the dice and put them in his pocket. Then he thought of the biggest number he could think of and added one to it. Having thought of a bigger biggest number, he added one again. He did this for a while.

And when the number filled his head completely, he both made and did not make a final addition. His head collapsed into a black hole, and the superfluities of his person were sucked inside.

V

1

As he entered the black hole by way of head, he left by way of ass. The fall was quick and he landed hard.

He was at the gates of a gothic mansion and its grounds. There was a party. Limousines and Ferraris drove up the drive and expelled a lace-and-kerchief congregation. They were pale and beautiful, dressed for grotesqueries and talking French. Above the mansion a purple moon glowed.

A woman stepped out of the shadows and into the purple glow of the moon. She wore a top hat and pantsuit and waved an ivory cane.

"Cherry?"

"Jim, you made it!" Cherry kissed him through the bars of the gate. "I wasn't sure you got my text."

"You texted me?" Jim took out his smart phone and saw that he had missed her text.

"Listen, I'm in a hurry. I've got to run. But I'll make sure you're on the list!" And Cherry ran off.

Jim climbed over the gate and walked up the drive. He felt strange in his presence, for he wasn't pale and beautiful, nor did he drive a Ferrari. Nevertheless, he walked up the drive to the mansion with the beautiful people and the Ferraris.

At the door to the mansion he saw the bald bespectacled man, who *was* kind.

"You!" he said. "Do you have any idea what you just

put me through? They shot me out of a cannon! I tried to transcend the essence of my being, but I just kept flying till I hit the brick wall at the edge of *paradise*. Einstein tells me it's all bullshit anyway, and then I get sucked into a black hole. My back hurts, I missed an important text, I may or may not be conscious, and it's all because of you. You *fucker*."

The bald bespectacled man said, "Hello, Jim. You're on the list." And he unchained the velvet rope that Jim might pass.

"That's it?"

"That's it."

And Jim became disarmed, for the bald bespectacled man *was* kind. "Well what is this place anyway?" he said.

"It's the devil's soiree. She throws it once a century. She calls it *Frankenmasque*."

"Lucy's here?"

"Among others."

So Jim crossed the threshold and entered *Frankenmasque*.

2

It was a grand entrance. Winding stairs chased macabre paintings up the stone walls. The carpets were red. A chandelier dropped dim light from the high ceiling. The pale and the beautiful mingled.

Jim looked for Cherry but he didn't see her. He looked for the devil too, but he didn't see *her*.

Now he felt more keenly the strangeness in his presence, for he beheld that the pale and beautiful people were also *sophisticated*. They drank wine with thumb and finger, spoke a great deal of French, and their laughter was jaded and ironic.

He thought, If there *were* a set of infinite Jims, I bet one of them would know how to talk to these people. Being not that Jim, he waited from a corner for something to happen.

Then the double doors beneath the winding stairs came open and there was an announcement. The pale and beautiful and *sophisticated* people filed through the doors and Jim followed.

In the next room there were many masked women. One by one they touched and took away the beautiful people until there was only Jim. The last masked woman touched him and he went with her.

3

They came to a small room. In its center there was a single chair bolted to the ground. The chair was equipped with restraints. An empty conveyor belt came in through one wall and left out another. The masked woman pointed to the chair and said,

"Sa-swa."

"What are you going to do to me?" said Jim.

"*Frankenmasque*. Voo lemur he. Sa-swa." She pointed to the chair.

"What is *Frankenmasque*?"

"Loo par-tea do diable."

"Diable. Yeah, I know it's Lucy's party. But what's with the chair?"

"*Frankenmasque*. Sa-swa."

So Jim sa-swa'd. The masked woman secured the restraints over his wrists, and over his ankles, over his chest. She flipped a switch on the wall and the conveyor belt moved. It carried into the room an assortment of human legs.

"Key pray-fairy voo?"

"Are those the legs of the beautiful people?"

"We. Key pray-fairy voo?"

"Uh, that one. Pray-fairy." He pointed with his head to a milky white leg. There was a black stiletto heel still strapped to the foot. "That's a nice one."

The masked woman removed from the belt the milky white leg and she held it up. With her face she made a question mark. Jim nodded. She went to the chair, pulled a lever, and Jim's left leg popped off.

"Fuck!" he said.

She replaced his left leg with the milky white leg with the stiletto heel. His own leg she placed upon the belt. She flipped the switch and the belt carried his leg away, and it brought some new legs *in*.

"Key pray-fairy voo?"

"Uh, no pray-fairy," said Jim. "Listen, I think there was a mix-up somewhere. I'm really not up for this shit right now."

She held up a leg dressed in slacks and a loafer. "Pray-fairy?"

"Fine. Whatever," Jim said.

The masked woman popped off his right leg and replaced it with the slacked and loafered leg. She placed his right leg upon the belt, flipped the switch, and the legs were carried away.

Now the belt brought into the room the assortment of arms. Jim chose for his left arm a plain and hairy arm, for it was near to his own. For his right arm he chose a tanned and muscular arm, which had around the bicep a *gnarly* tattoo.

His own arms were placed upon the belt. They became *among* the assortment and were carried away. Jim had now a milky leg with a stiletto heel, a leg of slacks and loafer, a left arm like his own and a right arm with muscles and a *gnarly* tattoo.

Now the belt brought into the room the assortment of torsos. Jim said, "Wait. Hold up a minute. Just, like, hold up. Are you really gonna rip out my chest? My heart's in there."

The masked woman said, "We." Then she ripped out his chest.

"Jesus!"

"Key pray-fairy voo?"

Upon the belt lay only the torsos of women. The breasts all jiggled as Jell-O cakes *jiggle*.

"Seriously?"

"Mall chance."

"Well, give me some perky ones."

The masked woman gave Jim a torso with perky breasts. His own torso was placed upon the belt, and it became *among* the assortment. The belt carried it away, and with it Jim's heart.

Now the belt brought into the room the assortment of pelvises.

"Not my fucking balls. You just got my heart, lady. Let me have my balls."

"*Frankenmasque*," she said. "Key pray-fairy voo?"

Jim chose for his balls the biggest balls on the belt. His own balls were placed upon the belt, and they became *among* the assortment. The belt carried them away, and with them Jim's dick.

Now the belt brought into the room the assortment of heads. But before Jim could make the final objection, he beheld among the heads *one* that was familiar. He said,

"Is that the beard of Billy Mays?"

The masked woman popped off Jim's head and replaced it with the head and beard of Billy Mays.

Jim's head she placed upon the belt, and it became *among* the assortment. The belt carried it away, and with it Jim's brain.

He watched it go. Jim watched his head leave the room. But he remained. He looked at the masked woman through the eyes over the beard of Billy Mays.

"Why am I me without my head?"

"*Frankenmasque*," she said.

4

So Jim came to the ballroom in the mansion of the devil. His left leg was milky and wore a stiletto heel, and his right leg was longer and loafered. One arm was like his own and the other was muscular with a *gnarly* tattoo. His breasts were perky and his balls were big, and the beard that he wore *was* the beard of Billy Mays.

The pale and the beautiful were likewise rearranged. Feminine eyes dared over masculine shoulders and uneven legs bore lopsided bodies. They wore no masks, for each was a phantom in a piecemeal shell of others. They mingled, danced, drank wine from trays with thumb and finger, and they laughed the jaded laughter.

Jim looked for his head but couldn't find it. He thought, If I see French coming out of my head's lips, I'm gonna break my own damn jaw.

Then he felt a hand touch the elbow of the arm that was like his own. He turned and beheld a thinly matched fellow with the head of a dark-eyed young woman.

"Jim?" the creature said.

He looked closer and saw in the dark eyes a spark. "Cherry?"

"We're not supposed to do this – like, acknowledge

each other – but I figure it's your first time. It's kinda freaky, huh?"

"Yeah. Kinda freaky. How did you know this was me?"

"It's the way you're looking around for your head. It's like, you're really confused, a little bit concerned, but you're alright about it at the same time. It's hard to explain. I like it though." She ran her fingers through the beard of Billy Mays. "And you *would* go for this beard."

"It's a pretty awesome beard," Jim said. He stroked the beard with the arm with the *gnarly* tattoo. "But is it *my* beard? I mean, am I me and I'm thinking with somebody else's brain, or are these somebody else's thoughts and I'm just sending them through? I can't shake the feeling that one of these assholes is messing up my head. Like, I'm gonna get it back and think I'm from Madrid or something."

"Honey, your head was messed up before you got here."

Then the lights became dim and everyone became silent. A balcony above the ballroom floor began to glow, there was a warbling *whoomf*, and Lucy appeared. She held to her face a glittering masque.

"Welcome to *Frankenmasque*," she said. "So many new faces tonight!"

This was met with jaded laughter. Jim didn't get it. Then he got it. He didn't laugh. He stroked the beard.

Lucy spoke with the airs of ritual, but her tone had a lightness that undercut the airs. Initiated pockets of the crowd replied in rote.

"Hearts of beasts and Grendel eyes, hearts that beat and wrestle whys."

"JAY SHWEE LOO EGGMAN!"

"What are you wearing under all that skin? Where do you end and I begin?"

"JAY SHWEE LOO EGGMAN!"

"Holes that bleed and poles that breed, coals that burn with awful need."

"JAY SHWEE LOO WALRUS!"

"Why are you hiding under all that skin? Open up and let me in."

"GOO GOO G'JOOB!"

The lights went up and Lucy vanished. Cherry put her thin fellow's arm through the arm that was like Jim's own. She whispered,

"You're never who you were, Jim, and you're never who you're going to be. This is just the madness between."

And *Frankenmasque* began.

5

He found a corner to lean upon and he observed from a distance the phantom squall. It was a dance without rule or rhythm. All the superfluities of personhood were mashed up and splayed across the ballroom floor. Consciousness lurked in the eyes that flashed in the twirl.

There was another man who leaned upon the corner. He was *entirely* a man, and he leaned with cool confidence.

Jim said to him, "Looking for your head?"

"My head is on my shoulders," the man said.

"How'd you manage that?"

"Crashed the gate. Here for a friend. We never leave a man down." The man sized Jim up with a glance. "You got a name, darling?"

"It used to be Jim. I'm not really sure anymore."

52

Jim played with his perky breasts. "I always kind of figured I was my head. Or at least my heart. Hell, balls ought to have *something* to do with it. You wouldn't happen to know the ontology of balls, would you?"

"I wouldn't. But I know a man has to fight for his name, and a man that used to be Jim is currently a bitch. So which is it, darling?"

Jim liked this guy. "Uh, Jim. Yeah, it's Jim then."

"You sure about that, darling?"

"Stop calling me darling."

"If you don't have a name and your heart's aflutter on the dance floor, you're everybody's darling. Darling."

Jim *really* liked this guy. Therefore he punched him with the arm that was like his own. "Call me darling again," he said.

And the man who was *entirely* a man said, "Ha! Maybe there's a man in there after all. Tell you what, Jim, forget about this place. Spare yourself the anguish, it's an empty burlesque. You want to know who you are, what a man is? A man is what he does, Jim. A man is what he does with his time and his sweat. A man is where he goes and who he fucks and what he says."

Jim considered this. "Well, before I came here I was at the edge of *paradise*. And the devil gave me a blowjob, like, right when I got here. And I told Kant he's a dick."

"That's more like it. So what it's going to be, Jim? You want to piss your panties in the corner, or you want to tag these bitches and get your balls back?"

"Balls."

"Alright, here's the deal. We've got a POW out on the dance floor. They're running the bulls on Cloud

Seven and his whore wife dragged him to this shit show. We're going in hard, a good old fashioned smash'n'grab. Get in, get what's yours, get out. We rendezvous at the gate."

And he pulled from the shadow of the corner a Louisville Slugger. With it he pointed to the balcony where the devil had *whoomfed.*

"You see that stack of human up there? That's Hunter. He's on point and he's bringing down the chandelier. When he does, me and Jack and Bunny are going in swinging."

"Wait," said Jim. He looked at the stack of human who *was* Hunter, and again at the man who was *entirely* a man. "What did you say your name was?"

"Ernest."

"Ernest *Hemingway?*"

"You in, darling?"

Jim took the bat.

6

Hunter leapt from the balcony to the chandelier. He wielded a sabre and he shook it at the phantoms in the ballroom. He said, "What I do, I do for Nixon." And he cut the rope and the chandelier crashed to the ballroom floor.

Then Hemingway charged in with a musket that was fitted with a bayonet. He was the first to strike, for he removed a pretty blonde head from a thick and veiny neck. Jack and Bunny were close behind. Jack cleaved with a machete, and Bunny swung a nine-iron.

Then Jim charged in with the Louisville Slugger. He made short work of several heads. The heads rolled on the floor and cursed in French. "Mayor-duh!" they said, and, "Vay-to-fay uncool!"

Hunter, the stack of human, climbed out from the ruin of the chandelier. He brandished the sabre and said, "Victory!" And he claimed an arm. "I am not a crook!" And he claimed three legs and a head.

So the pale and the beautiful were soon reduced to their wriggling parts. Hemingway and Hunter and Jack and Bunny sifted through the parts for the parts of their friend. Jim searched for himself. He found his head, and he found his arms and his legs and his chest. But he could *not* find his balls.

Then he heard a voice say, "Jim!" And he knew the voice. "Cherry!" And he found Cherry's head between four tits and a thigh. The spark in the eyes of the head *was* Cherry.

"You're back in your head!"

"Your balls." Cherry pointed with her eyes and Jim found his balls. "I kept them warm for you."

"You were wearing my balls?"

Cherry's head blushed. The heart in Jim's own chest, which he carried in the crook of the arm that was like his own, began to flutter.

"I'm sorry about your party," Jim said.

"Are you kidding? Best *Frankenmasque* ever. You should probably go, though."

For the wriggling parts of the pale and the beautiful were coming together, and the heads *were* cursing.

"Yeah. Um, I'll call you then."

"Yeah."

He ran out of the ballroom in the mansion of the devil, and he carried with him the superfluities of his person.

7

Jim reconstructed himself in a guest bathroom, and he was once more Jim from nub to skull. At the gates outside the mansion he came upon Hemingway and Hunter and Jack and Bunny, who reconstructed their friend.

When the work was finished, Hemingway said, "You in there, Fitzgerald?"

Fitzgerald blinked his eyes and shook his head. "You guys are insane," he said. "What did you do to her this time?"

Hemingway pulled Fitzgerald to his feet. "Your wife's a jack-fisted whore. Tonight we run with the bulls in the clouds and drink martinis until our tongues are dry and we can no longer speak. *Vamonos!*"

And Hemingway and Hunter and Jack and Bunny and Fitzgerald went down the drive. They climbed into a 1959 Cadillac Eldorado which had *metallic blue* paint and *tailfins*. Hunter took the wheel and Jack rode shotgun The others took the rear-facing backseat.

Jim waved. "Thank you, Mr. Hemingway! I got my balls back! And my head!"

"Looking good, Jim! *Paradise* is awesome, but it's only yours if you fight for it! So fight for it!"

"Don't listen to him," Fitzgerald said. "He only fights for lost causes. He thinks it's noble."

"*Vamonos!*"

Hunter lit a cigarette and the Cadillac peeled away.

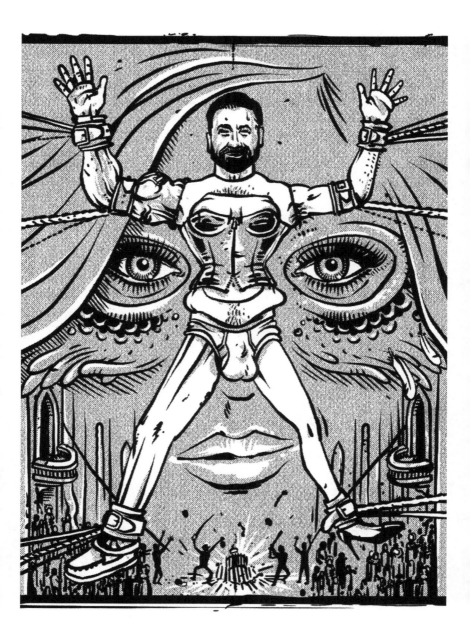

VI

1

So Jim *became* Jim. He was Jim in his heart, Jim in his head, and he was Jim in his balls. He was Jim *entirely.* He knew his Jimness for twenty-two years, and in those years he also experienced some *happiness.*

These are the brief *happinesses* of Jim in *paradise*:

He stepped up to the home plate at Fenway Park on two bad legs and he called his shot over the green monster. The slider came low and away and with a war-weary swing he pulled it down the line. He waved the ball fair and the ball sailed fair and over the monster, and it *was* a homerun. He hobbled to first, pumped his fist while rounding second, and he missed third altogether and hobbled back for the legal touch. Then he planted his feet at home and the big board said, Cubs Win! The tears of thirty-seven thousand Yankees were collected and fed to the goat who grazed at centerfield.

He put his eyes on the road and his hands upon the wheel and he rolled out to the great wide open. He smoked two joints and he kissed the sky. He listened for the songs that voices never shared. And when the black hole sun gently wept millions of peaches for the Bally table king, he wondered if he was paranoid or just stoned. For these *were* the words of the prophets and other tongues of lilting grace. And getting no satisfaction from the smoke of the ship on the horizon, he chopped down a mountain with the edge of his hand and said, Quinn the Eskimo was *here.*

He pushed his Deuce Coupe to one-forty on a back country road. The coppers flashed their lights in his dust. Crates full of jars of moonlight rattled in the backseat. The road ended where the canyon began, and there were no paths but dead on or capture. So he leaned out the suicide door and elucidated his convictions with a Chicago typewriter, raised a jar of the moon to the coppers, and said, "You'll never take me alive." He drank the moon and met the darkness in the canyon with a high five.

And his nights he spent with Cherry.

2

Then one day, while Jim cavorted through the aromas of Downtown, he came upon the angel who said fuck and laughed at suffering. The angel was handing out flyers to passersby, so Jim took one. He read,

Annual Cleopatra Lottery

Spend a night with the Egyptian Queen!

Enter in person at: 777 Lay Lady Lane.

Take your chances or accept your fate. Just don't be late!

The Cleopatra Lottery is run by the Paradise Grant Committee and is in full compliance with the Pussy Pact. All participants enter willingly and with full knowledge that their Indulgence Rights will be thoroughly abused.

Jim said to the angel, "Angel, hey. What is this?"

"It is what it says it is," the angel said.

"Yeah, but what *is* it?"

The angel looked at him and recognized him. "Oh, it's you. We run these things all the time. Winner of this one gets to bury his bone in the Queen of the Nile. You really haven't rolled for a scorcher yet?

You're not exactly fresh from the circus anymore."

"Been kind of busy," Jim said. "So if I win this I really get to lay Cleopatra?"

"Yep."

"What about this bit here? *Take your chances or accept your fate.* What does that mean? What's the difference?"

"You don't learn so quick, do you," the angel said. "Last time you asked me something like that, I heard they shot you out of a tiny cannon."

"Oh yeah." Jim checked the boulevard for philosophers. He saw none, so he said, "Give me a hint?"

The angel shrugged. Then he struck Jim in the face with his fist. It was a mighty strike, for the angel *was* an angel, and Jim fell upon the sidewalk.

"Dude. What the hell?"

And the angel said, "*Chance* is which hand I hit you with. *Fate* is when you hit the ground." Followed by a *chuckle*.

3

Lay Lady Lane was a long and shining broadway of neon lights and marquis that flashed the names of history's sexiest women. There were marquis for Marilyn Monroe, Mata Hari, Pocahontas, Jackie Kennedy, Audrey Hepburn, Madhubala, Nefertiti, Grace Kelly, Joan of Arc, and a thousand more. Above them all and at the center the name of Cleopatra glittered.

Jim went through the doors that revolved beneath the marquis. In the lobby there was the banter of hopeful men. Each man was queued in one of two lines: one line for men who took their chances, and one line for men who accepted their fate.

Jim went to the help desk. Behind it was a man whose nametag said, Butch, Angel in Training.

"First time?" said Butch.

"Yeah."

"Well, it's pretty simple. You go through that door, you get what's coming to you. You go through that one, you get something else. It's like, you walk the path or you roll the dice."

"Dice?" Jim checked his pocket. He still had the glossy red dice from the other side of the brick wall at the edge of *paradise*. "Seems like fate could do dice, too."

"Well, flip a coin, then."

Jim didn't *have* any coins, so he was forced to accept the redaction. "What about this part here? The part that says my indulgence rights will be thoroughly abused. I don't like the sound of that."

"Really?"

"What?"

"You're here for a chance to put your dick in the queen and you're asking me about the fine print."

"How do you know I'll do the chance thing?"

"From one guy to another, you don't exactly have the gravity of fate under you."

After some consideration, Jim decided that this was not an insult. "Indulge me," he said.

"Tell you what." Butch cracked his knuckles. "Here's the short of it. Lucy, her whole thing is everybody gets what they want, right? She hates rules. But what's the first thing you want to do when you get here? You want to fuck Cleopatra, that's what. So Cleopatra's got, like, a billion dudes playing Every Rose Has It's Thorn at her window, and that's a shit deal. For *everybody*. So she rounds up all the scorchers, you know, your Marilyn Monroes and your Marie Antoinettes, and they all march on Lucy. And Lucy's cool – have you met her? Yeah, you seem like the type. Anyway, they set up this whole infrastructure and assign teams of angels to field requests. It's all very organized. Now Cleopatra just gets an email every week, and she doesn't have to hear that damn song anymore.

"It all sounds good, except Cleopatra – just Cleopatra – needs a thousand angels to sift through all these requests. There's a shortage of angels. And there's a billion dudes that are pissed off about the selection process. They know damn well that Cleopatra isn't gonna blow some clerk from New Jersey. So there's hardly an angel in *paradise* that isn't reading love limericks, and everything with a dick is crying foul. It's a fucking mess.

"So Lucy comes out with the lottery and the Pussy Pact. She tells Cleopatra and every other scorcher that if they forego free will once a year and spread their legs for some Jack, she'll give them angelic privilege. That's, like, they get to be angels but they don't have to wear the uniform or do any work. And to the Jacks she says, Listen, you've got an eternity to win, and if you don't like it the Truth Road is that way. That cooled everybody off, and we built Lay Lady Lane."

And Jim said, "So this is just saying that I might not win."

"Pretty much."

"Thanks." And Jim went to take his chances.

4

The casino was filled with the men who did not have the gravity of fate under them. Though Jim did not count them, he thought that this was probably *most* men, for they were many. He wondered if accepting a light fate might have been better than taking a fat chance.

He rattled the glossy red dice in his pocket and looked for a craps game, but he couldn't find one. Nor could he find blackjack or poker or roulette or *any* slot machine. There wasn't even a bar. There weren't even hookers. It was the damnedest casino that Jim had ever seen.

But there *were* balloons. He came to understand that there was a balloon for every man, and inside a *single* balloon there was a ticket to Cleopatra's villa by the sea. So he mulled about through the fateless men and searched for his lucky balloon.

He mulled too long. Now there were only two balloons left. One of them was red, and the other was blue. He chose the blue, for it *was* the color of the sea. But as he chose it, another man chose it as well.

"This one is mine, thank you very much," said the irrelevant gentleman.

"I don't know," said Jim. "I think I touched it first."

"I mean to have it."

"Is there a moderator around here?"

As Jim looked around, the irrelevant gentleman tried to take the balloon. But Jim's grip was firm.

"Hey, that's not cool, man," he said.

"I have been coming to this lottery for two hundred years, and every year my balloon is blue. I mean to have it."

"I'll do you paper-rock-scissors for it."

"And take *two* chances while everyone else takes *one*? I am not an idiot, sir."

"I don't think that's how it works."

"Of course that's how it works. If the ticket is indeed in one of these two balloons, I will choose the correct balloon half of the time. And assuming that we are equally matched in the game of paper-rock-scissors, I will defeat you half of the time. To perform both in consequence requires a half times a half, and I am reduced to a quarter."

"But there's just two balloons."

"I will not trade my half for a quarter, sir. I mean to have this balloon."

"Yeah, but that doesn't make any sense. The ticket might be in the red one."

"So why don't you *take* the red one?"

"Well, maybe I will."

"Take it then."

"You know what, I'm *gonna*."

So Jim took the red balloon and the irrelevant gentleman took the blue. And now that every fateless man had chosen a balloon, the casino staff handed out the thumb tacks. There was some fanfare, and the owner of the casino thanked the devil for the Pussy Pact and all the fateless men for attending. Then he said, "May fortune fuck the queen!"

Jim took up the red balloon and the thumb tack and he popped the balloon. Inside of it was a ticket, and the ticket *was* to Cleopatra's villa by the sea.

So all but one of the fateless men became dejected. More dejected than any of them was the irrelevant gentleman. Jim put a consoling hand upon his shoulder and said,

"Cheer up, man. You're good luck."

5

Cleopatra answered the door in an old T-shirt and sweatpants. She ate pizza rolls from a ruby-studded chalice. She offered him one, so he ate it, and it was alright.

He said, "Are you Cleopatra?"

"The seventh," she said. "Daughter of kings, consort to Caesars, and Isis in the flesh."

"I'm Jim."

"Come in, Jim. And please, don't be shy. Or ceremonious. I loathe ceremonious. Just relax and enjoy yourself. Oh, and you're to take this, tuck it away, and you're not to open it until the contest is over."

"What is it?" Jim took the jeweled egg and turned it over in his hands. "It's very pretty."

"I'm not sure. I'm just the prize, as they say. Though they don't really say such things, do they? But come, this way. Fate is waiting in the sun room."

Jim put the egg in his pocket and followed Cleopatra through the villa by the sea. "I've heard a lot about you," he said.

"Oh, do tell me. What have you heard, my brave warrior of fortune?"

"Uh, well, you're the Queen of the Nile. You launched a thousand ships with your face. Um, you killed yourself with a snake because of Caesar. And you're, like, the most beautiful woman that ever lived."

Cleopatra took another pizza roll from the ruby-studded chalice. She talked while she chewed. "I was Pharaoh, never queen. It was the face of Helen of Troy that launched a thousand ships. The asp was invented by some sappy poet, and Mark Antony was never Caesar. And I could never get rid of the arm fat."

She wiped some pizza roll grease on her T-shirt then demonstrated the arm fat by the jiggling of her elbow. Jim saw that she *was* a bit flabby. But before he could assure her that she *wasn't*, she belched, and the moment passed.

"Don't take me the wrong way," she said. "I try not to be a bitch, but the mythology *does* get tiresome. And here we are. Fate awaits you, my brave warrior of fortune."

They entered the sun room. There was the flushing of a toilet, the grunting of a throat, and then a man came out of the bathroom. He was jagged handsome. He wore a tailored suit without a tie and his jet black hair was ice cold. He said to Cleopatra,

"Who's the interloper?"

"This is Jim," she said.

"Jim. Well, Jim, what do you say we dispense with the overture and get down to the movement? This is a lovely villa, and I'm sure you're fascinating company, but I'm double parked. And if the Pharaoh mouth-farts again I might lose my chub."

Jim recognized him. "Humphrey Bogart?"

"This isn't the beginning of a beautiful friendship, kid. Save the woo for the lady."

6

Cleopatra set three tattered board games upon the table. She said, "It's customary for the champion of fate to choose the final game. I've got The Game of Life, Connect Four, and Hungry Hungry Hippos."

Humphrey said, "Fate is the devil's word, it isn't mine. I don't want any part of it. It was my feet that got me through the door, and it's my disposition that'll get you in my car. Let the kid decide, he's good for it."

So Jim considered the games. He was adept at Connect Four, but it lacked the element of chance. Hungry Hungry Hippos was a silly game, and he doubted he could beat Humphrey Bogart at the Game of Life.

Then he remembered the glossy red dice from the other side of the wall at the edge of *paradise*. He took them out of his pocket and set them on the table. "I've got a better game," he said. "One roll, high roll wins."

"Short and sweet. I like the kid." Humphrey took up a die and he winked at Cleopatra. "But I have to warn you, Jim, the last time I rolled dice it was for eight thousand dinars, and the other guy died in the war."

"What the hell does that even mean?"

"It means I've been here before."

Humphrey rolled the glossy red die. It clattered across the table and came up two. Jim rolled *his* glossy red die. It clattered across the table and came up three.

"Ha!" Jim stood. "Eat shit, Bogart! The queen is mine!"

But Humphrey *was* cool. "Reel it in, cod-slayer. I'd say you should play it closer to the vest, but you wouldn't know how to wear one. And don't be a racist, the lady's a Pharaoh."

The Pharaoh belched. Humphrey stood and shook Jim's hand. Then he pulled Jim aside and spoke out of the Pharaoh's hearing.

"Between you and me, I'm just putting in an appearance here. It's for the papers. The gams on Cloud Nine suit me just fine. I'm happy for you. Really, I am. You're a good kid. Not too clever, but not too sweet either. It's a noble combination. That's why I didn't want to embarrass you in front of the lady."

"Embarrass me?"

"Joe Louis is taking a dive."

"What?"

"The Unknown Soldier, he's going for a walk."

"That isn't better."

"Your fly is down, kid. You're flopping around like a pygmy."

Jim flushed and he checked his fly. But his fly was *not* down. And in the time it took him to recover from his confusion, Humphrey hoisted the Pharaoh over his shoulder and kicked open a window.

"What the hell, man. You lost!"

Humphrey gave him a dramatic profile. "You had a good run, kid. It just wasn't meant to be." And he fired off a grappling gun and carried the Pharaoh away.

Jim ran to the window. Cleopatra waved. "Better luck next time, Jim!" she said. She jumped into Humphrey's Packard Super-Eight. Humphrey took her away, down the road that curved around the sea.

"But I won," Jim said.

He took out the jeweled egg and opened it. Inside there was voucher addressed to the runner-up in the Annual Cleopatra Lottery. Jim thought, How did she know? Then he thought, Oh, that *bitch.*

The voucher was for eighteen holes of golf with Adolf Hitler.

VII

1

"Fore!" Jim yelled. Even in *paradise* he hooked the damn ball. The ball sailed left over the fairway and past the bunker. It *thwunked* a tree.

"Ha!" Hitler pulled out his driver. "At least you're not trapped in the bunker. Get it?"

"Yeah, I get it."

Hitler teed up and took one practice swing. The swing was *creamy smooth*. When he struck the ball it went straight down the middle of the fairway. He said, "It was a suicide joke."

And Jim thought, Bogart is balls deep in the flesh of Isis, and I get hooks and Hitler jokes.

"You seem a little tense," Hitler said. "Perhaps you're unhappy with the lottery result." He replaced his driver and put an arm around Jim's shoulder. "Cleopatra and the Fuhrer have much in common. We will have a good time. And eighteen holes is more than she would have given you. Ha!"

"I get it."

"A sex joke!"

Jim climbed into the chariot with the Fuhrer. The chariot was drawn up the fairway by two *hipsters*, for their names were Larry Goldstein and Gary Steinberg.

"I'll bite," said Jim. "What could you possibly have in common with Cleopatra?"

Hitler said, "We ruled. We expanded our empires

until we were defeated by superpowers. We killed ourselves to avoid capture. Much in common."

"Yeah, but, I mean, with or without the arm fat she's smoking hot. She consorted with Caesars. And you were, like, the Lord of the Nazis."

"Fuhrer."

"It ain't the same."

They came to the place where Jim's ball *thwunked*. The *hipsters* set down the chariot, and they found the ball in some tall grass behind an oak tree. It was a fair lie. Jim took out a seven iron and he punched the ball into the fairway.

"The Pharaohs were not kind to their people," said Hitler.

"Dude. Nazis."

Jim exchanged the seven iron for a fairway wood and approached his ball. His swing was wild. The ball hooked and sailed out of play.

"You need to be more open," Hitler said.

"What?!"

"Your club face. You have to open up your club face."

"Oh, a golf joke."

"I never joke about golf."

Jim threw down the club.

"You killed a billion people. Like, a fucking billion. And you're giving me shit about my golf swing?"

"You have a terrible swing."

"Give me another ball."

So Hitler threw him another ball and he lined up for a second shot. "Relax your shoulders," Hitler said. "And bend your knees a little. Remember to keep your head down. You must strike the ball well before you can watch it fly."

Jim thought, The Fuhrer wants me to relax and be more open. He took a breath, opened up, and swung. The ball sailed straight down the fairway and thumped down on the fringe of the green. He handed his club to one of the *hipsters* as he climbed back into the chariot.

"It was Plato that showed me golf," Hitler said. "He is a very good teacher. Being more open, that was the first trick he showed me."

"You golf with Plato?"

"We have much in common."

"Go fuck yourself."

Hitler's drive was in the dead center of the fairway. He approached the ball with an eight iron. His swing was *creamy smooth* and he stuck the ball pin high.

"And it's not true about the billion people," he said.

"Well, I exaggerated a little," Jim said.

"In this place I've only killed one person. They only count it if you pull the trigger."

"Oh come on."

"It's true. I'm only credited with a single kill, one Adolf Hitler." He thumbed his chest. "You might call me a hero."

Hitler put his eight iron back into the bag and climbed back into the chariot. The *hipsters* carried on. Jim rummaged through his brain for some high school history.

"But how is that possible?" Jim said. "D-Day, the Battle of the Bulge, the concentration camps. That was all *you*. *You* made all that shit happen."

"Free will."

"Free will?"

"You're only responsible for what you *do*. According to the records, I just talked a lot. The kills all went to the people who listened to me."

"But you *forced* them to *do* it!"

"I thought so too. But you can't force anybody to anything. There is always a choice."

This was all too much for Jim. For not only was Hitler off the hook, but he got to be the guy that killed Hitler. When the *hipsters* set them down at the edge of the green, Jim took out his putter and pointed it at the Fuhrer.

"I don't buy it," he said. "And I don't care what the angels say. Adolf Hitler was an asshole." Then he three-putted for bogey.

"Just go to the Mortality Plaza," Hitler said. "It's on Corporeal Avenue, right downtown. That's where they keep the kill counts and the death records. They will tell you the same thing."

Hitler rattled home his putt. Jim took out the scorecard and wrote the scores. Around his six he drew a box. He circled Hitler's three.

"Well," Jim said, "at least an eagle can still put you six under."

Hitler slapped his shoulder. "Ha! A capital joke!"

2

The Mortality Plaza was huge. A building map in the lobby showed floors assigned to Haunting Holidays, Funeral Reenactments, Postmortem Vertigo and Trauma. Kill Counts and Death Stats was on the twenty-seventh floor.

And the twenty-seventh floor was packed tight with stacks of servers and processers. In the middle of the hum there was a woman at a desk. She made the *clacking* at a keyboard and her smile was Midwestern plaster.

"Kill Counts and Death Statistics," she said. "What can I do ya for?"

"Yeah," Jim said. "So, I was just golfing with Hitler, and he said I should come check this place out. He said he never killed anybody."

"Well now that just won't do, will it. Why don't you just take a seat right there and we'll sort this all out for ya. Does this Hitler have a full name?"

"What do you mean?"

"For example, maybe Hitler Stevens, or Hitler Robinson?"

"Adolf. Adolf Hitler. You don't know who Hitler is?"

And the woman made the *clacking* in the hum of the servers and processors.

"There he is. Well look at that. Adolf Hitler has one kill, and it's Adolf Hitler. What a coincidence."

"That's not possible."

"Our records are absolute and infallible. Look there, it even says so on my screen. Absolute and infallible."

"But he killed millions of people."

"Oh, I think I'd remember a seven figure kill count. Imagine that, seven figures. You'd have to wake up pretty early in the morning."

"Auschwitz. Look up Auschwitz."

And the woman made the *clacking* in the hum of the servers and processors.

"Oh, Nazi Deathcamp. That sounds exotic. You're certainly at the right place. I don't see any mention of an Adolf Hitler though. Let's see, I have a Rudolph Hoess down for sixteen thousand and forty-two.

Pretty impressive. And here's a Willhelm Boger, he's got a few thousand. There's an Oswald Kaduk with eight hundred and five. I don't see any millionaires."

"D-Day? The Russian front?"

And the woman made the *clacking* in the hum of the servers and processers.

"The highest kill count I have for D-Day is twelve hundred even. A man named Sam Anderson."

"Sam Anderson."

"That's right."

"Some guy named Sam Anderson killed more people than Hitler."

"A bunch more."

"That's retarded."

"Watch your language, mister. I don't know what you have against this Hitler person, but it's no reason to come down on the margins of society."

"Me?! But that's what he did! Like, big time."

"If you say so."

And Jim made the *guffaw* in the hum of the servers and processers. For his knowledge of high school history was depleted, and Hitler was still off the hook. He said to the woman with the plaster smile,

"Alright, so if Hitler's in the clear, and his henchmen aren't millionaires, all those kills had to go somewhere. So who's got them? Who killed the most people?"

She made the *clacking*. "Thomas Ferebee," she said.

"Who?"

"Says here he dropped a bomb on Japan. Two hundred eighty-seven thousand, five hundred and ninety-eight kills. That's a doozy."

"The pilot? They put that on the pilot?"

"Says here he was a bombardier."

"What about the guys that made the bomb? The inventor, the manufacturer? What about Congress and the President, the goddamn Kamikazes that started it?"

"Oh, we don't keep track of assists anymore."

"Why not?"

"Well, it turns out, what with all the going-on that goes about – ya know, the talking and the pushing – every kill had about a bazillion assists. Fried our computers to a crisp. We have a strict Kill/No-kill policy now. No moochers."

Jim made the *guffaw*. He thought, I'm gonna kill Humphrey Bogart. He said,

"I don't suppose that computer can tell me where Plato is."

"The philosopher?"

"Yeah."

"You'll have to go down to the Directory. It's about three blocks from here. There's a big rolodex on the roof, you can't miss it."

"Thanks."

"Have a good one."

3

Plato stood high on a cloud above the valley. In the valley there were pines and white rocks and a river, and there was a patch of wild flowers by the river and a big-horned antelope licked salt from the bank. Plato contemplated the valley from the cloud. He wrote some words in his notebook, and then a hawk came out of the sky.

Jim cleared his throat. He did not approach the

philosopher.

Plato said, "What do you think? Is it Valley?"

Jim said, "Yeah, it looks good. I like the hawk."

"Good, bad – who are we to judge? Is it Valley, or is it not Valley?"

"It definitely looks like a valley."

"Mmmmm. But what makes a valley *look* like a valley?"

So Jim *looked* at the valley. He said, "The mountains. The trees. The river."

"So a valley is the sum of these parts?"

"Sure."

"And without mountains there can be no valley?"

"Yeah."

"What, then, makes a mountain *look* like a mountain?"

He could pop this balloon by himself, Jim thought. He said, "Listen, the last time me and philosophy got together it didn't end so well. I'm done with it. My essence can go to hell. The reason I'm here, it's just been kind of a weird day, and I need this one thing from you. I know it's not your problem, but it's just one question. Please."

Plato nodded. "Mmmm. You are here because Hitler is off the hook."

"Uh, yeah. Wow. How did you know?"

"It happens a lot." Plato wrote some more words in his notebook, and salmon began to jump against the current of the river and a brown bear came out of the trees. "For some reason, the newly dead are perfectly happy until they find out that Hitler is happy too."

"Well?"

"Do you see that city, far off and floating in the clouds? That is my city, and it is the perfect form of the city. Its walls are graceful, its roads are wide and paved, its justice is noble. It is my masterpiece. Go there, and you will find your answer."

"How do I get there?"

Then Plato disrobed and Jim beheld the form of the philosopher. He was lean and wizened from nub to skull, but he *had* no genitalia. Instead, a French horn dangled between his legs. Before Jim could look away, the French horn flexed and blew out a solitary note.

Jim blinked. Plato neither moved nor spoke. The hawk screeched. Plato sucked in a breath and with a great effort he produced the cadences of Somewhere Over the Rainbow, and a rainbow climbed out of the French horn and *traversed* the sky. It settled at the gates of the perfect city that floated far off in the clouds.

"Just follow the rainbow," Plato said.

Jim no longer trusted philosophy, and he had his doubts about the French horn and the rainbow, but he needed an answer to the Hitler question. Therefore he stepped off the cloud and onto rainbow.

And he fell right through it. The ground of the valley in the shadow of Plato rushed up and kicked him in the head.

4

"Do you see your error now?" said Plato. For he stood beside Jim in the shadows of the valley.

"Error?" Jim rubbed the temples of his head with the palms of his hands. "The only error I made was coming here. I shoulda just said fuck it."

"Why did you *fall?*"

"I fell because you're a dick. You're all a bunch of

fucking dicks."

"Why did *you* fall?"

"I just want to know why Hitler's off the hook, man. It's a fair question."

"*Why* did you fall?"

"Because Cleopatra's a fat whore, Bogart's a goddamn cheat, and Hitler plays golf and tells jokes and is generally a pretty nice guy."

"Mmmmm." Plato shook his French horn and a few tired notes dribbled out. "I have an alternate theory."

"I'm all ears."

"You tried to enter an imaginary city by walking on the rainbow that I blew out of my cock. That's why you fell."

Jim waited for more, but there *was* no more.

"Get it?" Plato said.

"No, Plato, I don't get it."

"Mmmmm." Plato chewed the air. "Well, Hitler gets it. I suppose that's the important thing,"

And Plato walked out from the shadows in the valley of his shadow. The sun made the *glinting* upon his horn.

VIII

1

Jim became depressed. For though he was Jim in his heart, and Jim in his head, and Jim in his balls, he *had* no direction. He slept for seven years.

He wondered if a man could nap through eternity. He wondered if sadness was the jinx of free will, or the weight of an implacable environment. He wondered if his wondering was killing *paradise*.

One day, in the seventh year of sadness and napping, Jim received a text from Cherry. These are the texts that were exchanged between Jim and Cherry in the seventh year of sadness and napping:

Happy hundo Jim! ;)

hundo?

A hundred years! Lets party!

that was a hundred years?

The centennial man. So what's it gonna be? I say we get a bucket full of coke and duck till we're insane.

*fuck

i don't think i'm up for it

I'll bring some more girls.

na u go ahead I'm tired

What's up with you lately?

just taking a break

I know what you need.

don't

Too late! :P

dammit

I know how you can thank me.

i don't even know what u did

I want you to nuke my pussy.

2

The door to Jim's bedroom banged open. He sat up and blinked away the fuzz of years. A wild man with shining eyes grabbed him by the ankles and pulled him off the bed. His head bounced on the floor.

"Art thou Jim?" the wild man said.

Jim blinked away the fuzz of the bounce. "I art," he said.

The wild man picked up the bed and threw it out the window. Glass shattered. The frame of the bed clattered on the walk below. The mattress hung in the window, for it was *impaled* by a shard of glass.

"Then I am Marco Polo." He kicked over the night stand. "And you are fortunate in the company you keep. I am neither cheap nor easily persuaded."

With a fist he made three neat holes in the wall. Then he unzipped his trousers and began to piss in the corner. He spoke over his shoulder while he pissed.

"You have three minutes to dress yourself. In that time you will also pack a single bag. The bag may not weigh more than a stone, and it ought to contain clothing for all seasons and terrain."

"I'm not packing a bag," Jim said. "Did Cherry send you? Tell her she owes me a bed. I'm not going anywhere. I don't care about the years. I just need to sleep for a while."

"Two minutes and forty-two seconds." Marco shook and zipped and then he kicked another hole in the wall. He tore the light fixture from the ceiling and smashed it on the floor.

"Please stop doing that," Jim said.

"Two minutes and fifteen seconds." Marco pulled the flatscreen from the wall and cracked it over his knee. He threw the remains out the window, along with a lamp and a chair.

"Alright," Jim said. "I'm getting up. I'm up, alright? Just give me a second here. I'll take a shower and get my shit together. Like, half an hour. I'll go. I'm going. You hear me? Just let me get sorted, you psycho."

"Too late." Marco grabbed Jim by the shoulders. "Look at this place. It's untenable. I've scheduled it for demolition. One minute."

"You what?!"

And Marco walked out the door. Jim struggled into a pair of jeans and stumbled after him.

"What does that mean, demolition? You're not serious. I like this house. What's wrong with a house? People live in houses. Goddammit."

When he breached the front door the white wall of daylight staggered him. Marco pulled him out to the edge of the property. Then a tank rolled through the fence and onto the yard and Marco gave it a thumbs up. The tank fired a shell and the house exploded. The tank fired another shell and the house fell over. Jim thought the third shell was probably gratuitous.

"This isn't funny," he said. "I was just taking some time off, man. Is it a crime to get sad once in a while? I had stuff in there."

The eyes of Marco shined. "Was it the stuff of dreams, Jim? The stuff of adventure? Did it smell like the dead salt of acrid seas or the sour sweat of the jungle? Was it a fist raised against winter and the hot blood of glory?"

Jim swallowed. "Uh, no. It was, like, albums and stuff."

"Art thou yet a man?"

"I don't know."

"Sign this."

"What is it?"

"Sign it."

Jim signed it.

"It's settled, then. We hoist sail at midday."

3

So Jim sailed with Marco into the *bleakness*. The waters were calm and shrouded. Then they became choppy and the shroud began to lift and Jim beheld the dark wall of storm.

"Is that where we're going?" he said.

Marco heaved the wheel of the ship. "To the mountain behind it."

"Can't we go around?"

"There is only one way through the storm. There is only one way up the mountain."

"What's the point? We're already dead."

"That's why they call it the Stupid Fucking Mountain." Marco steered the ship head on and into crush of the rising waves. The ship climbed and crashed and climbed again. "No man has a reason to climb it, yet all men *must*. And after the climbing, in spite of all sanguinity, you find that the top is just another rock."

"So what's the point, man? What's the difference between taking a nap and climbing a stupid fucking mountain?"

"*The* Stupid Fucking Mountain."

They came upon the storm and the storm came upon them. Jim clung to a crossbeam. Marco commanded the helm. Waves and rains and winds of storm tossed the ship that moved through the *bleakness.*

Then the waters were calm again. The crags of the base of the mountain rose out of the waters and climbed into the shroud of distance. Jim looked long at the shroud.

"How tall is it?" he said.

"It's never been measured." Marco dropped anchor and lowered the mainsail. He cut loose a lifeboat that splashed down in the waters. "And you wouldn't be the first to try. Just remember to keep going up."

"I really don't feel like climbing it."

"You *must* climb it."

"Yeah, I don't think I'm gonna."

Marco gave Jim the thing that Jim had signed. "Read the last paragraph," he said.

So Jim read,

The undersigned hereby agrees that, upon failure to reach the peak of the Stupid Fucking Mountain in full compliance with the rules stated above, all freedoms shall be forfeit for one year and one day, during which period the undersigned shall be placed into the custody of lechers and psychotics and sadists. The undersigned shall have experiences including, but not limited to: rape, torture, and mutilation.

"You're bluffing," Jim said.

The eyes of Marco shined. "Then call it," he said.

Jim stepped into the lifeboat.

4

So Jim climbed up the Stupid Fucking Mountain. It was also a *big* fucking mountain, and he climbed for many months. His shoes wore out and his feet became hard. His jeans and his T-shirt withered and his skin become rough. His hands became strong.

He thought, Man this sucks.

Then a sound from the *bleakness* came to him. He searched for it. He found a young man who sat in a shallow cave and played a haggard guitar. Blonde hair hid the edges of his face as he strummed with brutal sincerity.

The young man looked up and moved the hair from his eyes. Jim knew his eyes, just as he knew his sound.

"Hi," Cobain said.

"Hey," Jim said. He stepped with caution, for he felt like a gazelle coming upon a lion. "I, uh, heard you playing."

Cobain ran his fingers over the haggard body of the guitar. "I never thought I'd play again," he said. "Everything got so fucked up the first time around. But there's something about this place. The *bleakness*. Like, this guitar, I hacked the wood for the body out of a tree with a sharp rock. The tuning pegs are hawk bones. The strings are guts. It's the best guitar I ever played."

Jim sat down on a bare rock in the shallow cave. Cobain strummed his guitar. The cave reverberated the imperfections of the sound and the *bleakness* hid in the cracks of the mountain.

"It's raw," Jim said.

Cobain moved the hair from his eyes. "It's strange. When you get everything you've got nothing. I had everything once, and then *paradise* was just everything all over again. It took somebody to come along and take it all away, and now I've got something again." He played a single chord. "I got raw again."

"Can I ask you something? I guess it's kind of personal."

"That's alright."

"Why did you kill yourself?"

A smile played between Cobain's teeth. "It seemed important at the time," he said. "And there was a lot of pain. The useless kind of pain, the kind that just sits in your head and makes you heavy and takes the color out of everything. It makes you ugly. I guess the worst part is being able to see how ugly you've gotten, and not being able to do anything about it. So I did something about it." He turned a hawk-bone peg and the tone of the deepest gut-string fell. "I didn't kill myself for any special reason. I killed myself because I wanted to die."

Jim tried to think of something to say. He couldn't. Then Cobain said,

"It was crazy to see it. I just expected darkness. Then I was standing there over my body, looking at the chunks of my brain mashed into the ceiling. Like, the mess never occurred to me. The pain was all cerebral. Metaphysical. Seeing your metaphysics splattered around the room, gushing out of the back of your head, it's a pretty harsh trip.

"But what really fucked with me was when the angel popped up next to me. He said, I bet you'd have written a kick-ass song about that."

"Did you?"

Cobain plucked a few notes. "It's a little rough around the edges," he said.

And he played a song.

5

The peak of the Stupid Fucking Mountain *was* just another rock. Jim kicked it down the side of the mountain and watched it roll. With the song of Cobain in his head he showed his balls to the *bleakness,* and his heart drummed four beats at a measure.

He pulled out his smart phone and texted to Cherry,

the nuke is hot

IX

1

Paradise lay flat and gray. Ashes fell from the mushroom cloud and made a quiet blanket on the ground.

Jim looked at his dick. "How many megatons was that?"

"I don't know, but I can't move," Cherry said. Her breasts were soft and pink beneath the fallout. Her blasted pussy murmured queefs that stirred the ashes.

Jim thought, When she does move, she'll leave an angel in those ashes. He kissed her on the forehead. Then he stood and stretched. He wanted a sandwich, but he doubted any sandwiches survived.

"Did we overdo it?" he said.

"Water," Cherry said.

"I don't see any water."

"I'm so thirsty."

Jim looked out over the flatness and the grayness. There was nothing, and he beheld *it*. Then a jagged light broke the sky and it ripped through the air like lightning. The atomic flakes shuddered in the waves of the ripping. A tremor swam through the ground.

"No more," Cherry said.

"That wasn't me."

Then there was a warbling *whoomf*. A hole came into the world and the devil walked out of it. Jim thought for a moment that she had painted her face, but the black lines were mascara. She was crying.

2

"They are so cruel to me," she said. "Why are they so cruel? What have I ever done but give them freedom and happiness? By what rights do they accuse me? I work so *hard.*"

Her voice quivered. Her hands shook. There was rage as well as sadness. Jim took two backward steps, for he was terrified of emotional women, and *this* one was the devil. He looked to Cherry, but Cherry was blasted and far away.

The devil walked at him. Jim thought that he'd finally gone and done it and that *paradise* was over. He thought he was about to feel some hell. Instead, she buried her face in his neck and wept.

"What am I going to do?" she said. "What can I do, Jim? The firmament is broken. There will be war. I hate the wars of men. It's the blood, I can't stand it."

Jim held her close and said, "It's okay." Because sometimes it worked with *other* girls.

"I give and I give and I give and it's never enough or maybe it's too much I don't know I just work so hard and now everybody's going to hate me. They're going to hate me all over again and all I ever did was give them everything they ever wanted and they won't stop they'll hate and kill until it's all gone everything I've worked for."

Jim stroked her hair and said, "Shhhhh."

Another tremor swam through the ground and the jagged light flared.

Jim said, "Was it something *I* did?"

Lucy pulled her face from his neck. She set her eyes into his. She was beautiful and timeless and bleary. Her hand upon his cheek put warmth in his bones.

"*Jim*," she said. "So reckless and innocent. It was the nuke. It ripped open the firmament."

"I'm sorry."

She kissed him. He kissed her back. It was a reflex. When it was over Lucy laughed at his shock. She wiped the mascara from her eyes.

"I'm quite the devil, aren't I?"

"You're a beautiful devil."

"And you're very sweet."

"Did I really break *paradise*?"

"*Paradise* is yours to break."

"Uhgghh," Cherry said. "*No more.*"

The rebuke stabbed Lucy in the chest. She staggered. She took a breath. Then she closed her eyes and opened different ones.

"The slut is right," she said. "I built these firmaments. I can fix this."

Her transformation was swift. There was a *whoomf* and Jim stood before a professional woman in white heels, skirt, and blazer. And he saw that he was also professional, for his superfluities were draped in a suit and tie. He made a question mark with his face.

"You're going to help me," Lucy said.

"I still don't understand what's broken."

"Your nuke made a crack in one of the firmaments. And now all the zealots of all the denominations of Christianity can see each other."

This didn't make enough sense to Jim. He furrowed the question mark.

"They needed to gloat, so I let them gloat," Lucy said. "They were all very special until about ten minutes ago. They will not like this new equality."

Jim looked at his tie. He flopped it around. "I don't know," he said. "I don't think I'm cut out for this. Can't you just get Jesus to talk to them?"

"He retired."

"What?! Why?"

"You're about to find out."

Lucy checked her complexion in a pocket mirror. Behind her the air shimmered and warbled and a hole came into the world. "And Jim, they know me as Gabriella. Say nothing about the devil."

"Okay," Jim said. "Wait. Which *are* you?"

Her smile was coy. They went through the hole.

3

The cloud was furnished with a round table and some chairs. In the chairs sat Martin Luther, Pope John XX, King Henry VIII, Saint Paul, and Joseph Smith. Gabriella claimed the final chair and Jim stood a safe distance behind.

"Thank you for coming," Gabriella said. Her white blazer glimmered. "You are all aware of this by now, but I will say it plainly so there is no mistake. Everybody goes to heaven, and heaven is uniformly pleasant throughout."

There was some silence. King Henry coughed but his heart was not in *it*. Martin Luther stood. He said,

"Let me be the first to welcome this news, and to praise God in His mercy and His wisdom. It brings joy to my heart that the entirety of the human spirit is given this plane to thrive upon. I have ever contended for a democratic eternity, tempered by the dominion of a merciful Master, and all Protestants glory in this new brotherhood."

Luther retrieved a stack of papers from under his chair. He *thudded* them upon the table. The stack was three feet high.

"And I formally submit this petition, signed by one hundred millions, demanding that the Catholics be evicted immediately."

"*Hurrrr hurrrr hurrrr.*" Pope John XX laughed. "One hundred millions. *Hurrrr hurrrr hurrrr.*"

"They are honest millions! I would take any one among them against all your corrupted legions!"

Gabriella accepted the petition and she coaxed Luther back into his chair. She informed everyone that there would be no evictions.

"Everybody goes to heaven," she said. "It was decided a long time ago that Earth is a hard place with an obstructed view, and it's unfair to expect its inhabitants to get anything right. If entry were contingent upon rightness, the place would be empty. Every one of you is here because none of you are right."

"Proverbs thirteen verse three," said Saint Paul. "He that keepeth his mouth keepeth his life; but he that openeth his lips shall have destruction."

"Very good, Paul," Gabriella said. She threw him a treat and he ate it. "It may have been a mistake to veil this relativism. It may be that the orders of angels have purchased your happiness with an awful hubris. But the firmaments were built and you were given your time to gloat. That time is finished. Now that you see one another you have two options: Join together and celebrate your mutual failings, or fight for nothing."

"Hubris," said the Pope. "*Hurrrr hurrrr hurrrr.*"

"This man cannot be retained in heaven!" Luther said. "King Henry, surely you have no love for these vicars."

"Ay, these wonky twats been on the piss for yonks," King Henry said. "All smart for God but they go arse over tit for an Irish penny. Never been a Pope that didn't beggar the poor cunts that fagged around for him. Give England a sword if it's a buggered Pope that stiffs you."

"What?"

"It means *ay*. Fuck Rome."

"*Hurrrr hurrrr hurrrr.*"

"Imposter!" The word came hot from the mouth of Joseph Smith. "There is no Pope John Twenty," he said. He stood and brandished his tablet high. "It says right here on Wikipedia. There is a Pope John Nineteen, a Pope John Twenty-one, but due to a counting error there is no Pope John Twenty!"

"Ha!" King Henry pounded the table with his fist. "Counting Popes is a mug's game, any road. Can't build a cathedral with holy bell-ends. Fuck the Popes, count the shillings! Yaa haa harr!"

"ENOUGH!"

Gabriella unleashed her beauty and her fury. She diminished *all*.

"Are these trivialities not yet beneath you?" she said. "Even here, in the seats of *paradise*, will you squabble over small ideas and circumstantial prejudice? Existence itself stretches out before you in all of its eternal possibility, and this is where you sit, and these are your discussions. The world that sorrowed you is a drop in the ocean. In recompense I give you the ocean, and you fight over the drop."

Jim thought, I can't believe this is the same woman that welcomed me to *paradise* with a blowjob.

She said, "There is only one question that should concern you: Why must angels lie to keep the peace in heaven?"

The air shimmered and warbled. Devil or angel, she stepped through hole. And Jim stood forgotten on the cloud of war that he had nutted.

4

Then Joseph Smith pounced on the vicar and snatched off his hat. There was nothing underneath it.

"Har! Pope Fishbowl the First!" King Henry said.

Smith peered into the cavity of the papal cap. "There's something in here," he said. The papal cap echoed, *something in here, in here, hurrrr.*

Luther said, "If you pull another Testament out of that hat, I'll see that you eat every doorbell in *paradise.*"

Smith reached into the papal cap. It required the full length of his arm. And when he withdrew his hand it held a single sheet of wide-ruled notebook paper. He read,

"By the time you read this, we will have won the war. *Hurrrr hurrrr hurrrr.*"

"It's a rouse!" Luther jumped from his chair.

"Sabbing bastards!" King Henry drew his sword. He struck down the falsely numbered Pope.

Luther whistled and a silver osprey flew forth. "Black smoke!" he said. He leapt upon the bird. "Black smoke!" He flew.

Smith unchained his bicycle and pedaled away.

King Henry mounted his steed. He approached Jim with sword drawn and gave Jim a nod. "That's a right stonker in those yankee breeches," he said. "Wield it for England and I'll grant you all the fadges north of Leeds."

"What? I mean, no thanks," Jim said.

So the king insulted him severally and galloped off. Only Saint Paul remained at the round table. He sat with his head bowed and his hands clasped before him. He said,

"Corinthians six, verse three: Know ye not that we shall judge the angels?"

"I don't have any treats," Jim said.

The saint let fall a single tear. And somewhere below, on the lower planes of *paradise*, Jim heard the first shots of the war.

5

This is Christopher Hitchens, reporting dead from the godless soup of eternity. Approximately ten hours ago – ten hours relative to *what* remains unclear – the atomic ejaculate of a Tennessee man cracked the Christian firmament and the myriad zealots of Christ are swarming. The nest has been stirred, comrades and friends, and they've taken to the clouds with Bible, fist, and tongue. The Bible, one supposes, is for bludgeoning; the fist is a reminder – a rather pedestrian one – of the glory of the ever-vacationing Jehovah; and the purpose of the Christian tongue remains scientifically mysterious. If it's on your bucket list, as impossible as such a list may seem in this Cartesian infinity – but if you have one, and it includes proselytization or purification, catechism or communion, inculcation or inquisition, this is the place to be.

And I have the dubious honor of interviewing the man that frenzied these ridiculous sheep – these sadomasochistic and sexually inverted apes. Jim, thanks for dropping in.

Yeah. No problem.

You look pretty good for the epicenter of a holy war.

Thanks.

Do you have a god in the race, Jim?

Uh, no. I was never religious. My aunt was a Baptist. I wouldn't bet on the Baptists.

To bet on any particular sect of this deranged cult, of this outdated menagerie of demagogues and faith-mongers – it's a bet on a lame horse. A dead horse. A dead lame and plaintive horse. Only the religious would make it.

I guess they might. Or they do.

I have it here that you were even present for the diplomacies.

I was.

Well? Perhaps you could give us the upshot.

I'm still trying to wrap my head around it, man.

Give us the old college try.

Alright, well uh, the devil, or I mean not the devil. Gabriella. I don't know, I think she's transgender. She came to me in tears and said me and Cherry put a crack in the firmament. Evidently the angels put up this firmament so the different kinds of Christians couldn't see each other. That's part of their *paradise*, I guess, is knowing they're the ones that got it right. Cherry's the girl I'm seeing, by the way. As far as you can see a girl around here. Anyway, we had this epic fifteen-rounder and we blasted a hole in the firmament. Gabriella tells me I have to help her fix it. So we *whoomf* on over to the cloud where they're doing the diplomacies and Gabriella gives these guys the bad news. You know, that *paradise* is for everybody and there's a lot of relativism going around. They weren't too happy about that. So Gabriella tells them there's a whole ocean to swim around in and they're just fighting over a drop. Which, like, totally floored me, but it went right past these guys. They didn't give two shits, man. It turned out that the Catholics were playing dirty, anyway, so none of it really even mattered. Everything just went to hell.

What an utterly useless response. If it was of any importance I'd call it tragic. To those of you still with us, I salute your resilience and I'm humbled by your endurance. I'll try to reward it with a retelling – with an editorial – more worthy of your auditory canals. Though I doubt the irony can be missed by anybody, there are some important subtleties that might escape the first glance. It's fairly well established – the one-two punch of sexual repression and deviancy that infests the institutions of religion – Hey! You can't come in here! I am a journalist. We are protected under international –

6

The Anglican sheathed his sword, apologized to Jim for the intrusion, and departed. Christopher's head lay on the desk next to a decanter of red wine and a half-empty glass. His body lay on the floor.

"I'm under the impression he hasn't read the articles of the Geneva Convention," Christopher's head said.

Outside the makeshift studio there were the *clangs* and *bangs* of war. Jim heard the thunder of the hooves of cavalry charge into the booms of modern artillery. He heard trumpets battle drums and megaphone Revelations.

Christopher's head bit at the stem of the half-empty wine glass. But without hands he could not *get at* the wine. Jim thought, Nobody up here is going to die.

"Are they going to fight forever?" he said.

"Oh, I'm sure they'll come to an accord before eternity's end," Christopher's head said. "Even the religious can't escape the strangeness of infinity. If it can happen, it will." He curled his tongue around the stem, yawed back and forth, then gave up. "Do me a favor?"

Jim picked up the glass and poured the wine into the head's mouth. He said, "Why can't they all just be special together?"

"The war of the ages is being fought all around me, and I'm trapped in a windowless room with a pacifist," Christopher's head said. "Let me try it this way. We're pattern-seekers, Jim. Nothing thrills us more than the seventh note of the scale followed by the eighth. It's coded into our genetics through a hundred thousand years of survival and evolution. To understand the world is to manufacture order out of chaos. But – how did you put it? – with all this relativism going around, order isn't so easy to manufacture. And in the absence of order, the reptilian brain will smash a million square pegs through the proverbial round hole. You're simple so I'll put it even more plainly: These men invented God that they might shovel their doubts up his ass, and your coital nuke stabbed him in the guts and now it's raining shit."

"Pattern seekers?"

"Fuck me."

"Well, help me out, then. Because what you just laid out sounds like a pattern."

"Some patterns exist. A few examples of false pattern recognition don't convict the thought processes of the entire species."

"You're an atheist."

"By default."

"So where do the angels fit in? The clouds and eternity? Afterlife? An atheist in *paradise* is a contradiction."

"I have certain suspicions in that regard. The ever-expanding thought-reality of this place is reminiscent of Lewis: *Hell is a state of mind.* I'm sure even you've heard that before. This freedom-loving devil sounds an awful lot like she walked out of the pages of Paradise Lost, and all this gallivanting around with dead celebrities is straight out of the pages of Dante. *Nel mezzo del cammin di nostra vita.* I scarcely need mention the central conflict, this Paradise-sans-Truth tension, a trope as old and quaint as Eden. Throw in the haphazard philosophies, the hipster irony, the cheap jokes – It's almost as if some publicly educated and under-employed ass is having literary spasms."

The eyes of Christopher's head roamed about the studio until they found the place where the studio met the page. And they looked up off the page and at *me*. I looked away, for I *was* guilty. I stepped outside and I smoked a cigarette. I poured myself another coffee. I thought about giving up. But I really wanted to know how Jim was going to fix the firmament, so I went back. I expected to martyr myself against the edges of Christopher's rhetoric, but when I sat back down he had already moved on.

"As for the angels," he said, "If apes can graduate, so too can men. It would be a cosmic travesty if we were evolution's final product."

"So everybody's got a pattern for everything," Jim said. He stole a drink from the half-empty glass, and he nearly spit it back out. "Ughh, that's bitter."

"It's Amarone."

"It's bitter." Jim set down the glass. "So what do we do? Nothing? Just pull up a chair and mock what passes?"

"Carry me," Christopher said.

"What?"

"I don't need a body to give these demagogues what-for. Even the invicted heart draws blood from the brain. We'll divest them of these superstitions with reason, with the dynamics of logic and argument. We'll scour the fields of battle with the ink of a thousand years of secular thought. Carry me, Jim! I'll eat in *paradise* what I merely disdained on Earth."

"I don't think it will work," Jim said.

"Carry me," the head said.

Jim squatted and met Christopher's gaze with his own. He said, "These religious guys might be a little silly, but Immanuel Kant is a fucking *dick*." Then he made for the door.

"Jim! What humanity lost through submission it will win back through progress and irony! Mark those words, Jim. One day!"

7

So Jim wandered upon the fields of battle. While he wandered he beheld many feats of violence and insanity. He saw the pointy hat of a bishop that wobbled in the hatch of a Sherman tank, and the tank rolled at the head of a legion armed with shovels and pitchforks. He saw great volleys of arrows exchanged between clouds. He saw the shells of artillery rip into a battalion whose armor was duct tape and Bible paper.

And the angels kept a loose perimeter in the sky and on the ground. Some of them were confused or concerned, but most of them pointed and laughed and had a pretty good time.

The crack in the firmament streaked over the war. It glowed.

It came to pass that Jim came to a place between three hills. The place was sheltered by trees and a river. It was open and flat, occupied by a peaceful throng. A middle-aged woman in a conservative summer dress met him as he entered.

"Welcome," she said.

"What's going on here?" Jim said. "There's a war going on, you know."

"Well, we are the Presbyterian Church of Canada, and we'd much rather have a picnic. Would you like some juice or some coffee? There will be cake and cookies afterwards, but you're welcome to some coffee now. I could introduce you to the boys. Oh, excuse me. *Men.* You're not boys anymore, are you? My son is about your age."

"Afterwards? After what?" Jim made his suspicions known with a *squint.*

"Oh, we have a very special speaker." Then she leaned in and spoke confidentially. "It's top secret, but I'll give you a hint. His name is John Calvin."

The name didn't mean anything to Jim, but he understood from her tone that it *was* impressive. "Holy buckets," he said. He retained the *squint.*

"The holiest," she said. "Can I bring you to my son? The two of you will get on just great."

"Sure."

She led him to a small group of *men* at the edge of the peaceful throng. She introduced them and Jim introduced himself and then she left. Her son had thick shoulders and a good handshake. His name was Michael. Jim liked him, and the liking intensified his suspicions.

"So Jim," Michael said, "Are you looking to buy something, or just hiding from the weather?"

"What do you mean?"

"I mean, do you have any interest in becoming a Presbyterian?"

"Oh, well, not really. I'm not very religious."

"That's quite alright, Jim. No worries, really. You know, I've got this theory about Jesus. Not sure how original it is, but it goes like this: Don't shove Him down anybody's throat, and He won't fly out of anybody's ass." He slapped Jim on the shoulder. "You alright? Looks like you've got something in your eye."

For Jim had *squinted* too far. He relaxed his face.

"You seem alright," he said.

"Yeah, I know we get a bad rap once in a while. Hell, we deserve it. And I'll be honest with you, I only believe in half of this stuff myself. But I really *do* believe in that half."

"Which half?"

"Redemption. The idea that no matter what you've done, you can come back around. You can get clean and be good in the eyes of God. Like, we all fuck up sometimes, you know? And sometimes it gets pretty ugly. But you can always come back here, and as long as you come with an open heart, you can get back to even."

Jim considered these words, for he *had* nuked the firmament, and he felt pretty bad about it. And the peaceful throng *was* nice and wholesome. They would probably even forgive him.

Maybe I'm a Presbyterian, he thought.

John Calvin arrived. He elevated himself on a tree stump in the center of the throng. He spoke for twenty minutes. He condemned the war but not those who fought in it, and he asked everyone to pray for their misguided brothers and sisters. He spoke eloquently about the difficulties of moral absolutes and the mysteries of eternity. As he neared the end of his speaking, he said there remained a single theological problem to resolve, and Jim was hanging on his words.

Calvin said, "As we know, God in His wisdom and His mercy granted Grace Everlasting to some of us, and Damnation to others. We are all mortally bound to the Original Sin and we share equally in the depravity of the Human Condition, and His choice has nothing to do with our little worlds, and everything to do with His mercy. The difficulty we face, following the crack in the firmament, is that everyone is now in Paradise. It has been theologically established that this is not the will of the Creator, and something must be done.

"Lacking the authority to deliver Damnation, and being naturally opposed to it for the frailty of our Condition, there is but one path to Reconciliation with God. Some of our number must reject Paradise through voluntary discomfiture. The discomfort must not be too severe, for through pride and vanity we would flay ourselves and abuse God's dignity. Nor must it be too trifling, for through gluttony we would abuse His mercy. Therefore, one third of our number must wear scratchy undergarments and abstain from wi-fi for the duration of the breach of the firmament. We shall endure this discomfiture together, in rotation, in shifts not less than twelve and not exceeding forty days. We thank God for His patience and for giving us this wisdom. Amen.

"Oh, and if anyone has a skin condition, or is otherwise ill-disposed to the wearing of scratchy undergarments, please give your name to Mrs. Roy. We'll find you a more suitable discomfiture."

Michael stopped Jim at the exit. "Jim!" he said. "At least stay for some cake!"

"It's too sweet," Jim said.

8

She sat in a mortar hole in the charred and blasted ground. Light played upon her through the branches of a broken tree. She was Gabriella where the light touched her, and she was Lucy in the shade.

"They love this war," she said. "They love it more than the lie. They will never stop fighting."

Jim sat down next to her. He was unsure about their relationship, for she was both the devil who had blown him and the angel who had harangued the Christian elite. He said, "It's the ones that aren't fighting that you should be worried about. They're itching to go to hell." But it was a *feeble* joke, and it fell upon the blasted ground and died.

"Would I lie to you, Jim?" she said.

"I don't know."

"If I did, would you be angry? If the lie gave you *paradise*, if it gave you everything you ever dreamed of, would you still be angry?"

"I guess so."

"Why?"

"I mean, things are either real or they aren't. You want things to be real."

There was some silence. Jim watched the light play upon the angel and the shade upon the devil. He found in his pocket the card she had given him when they first met. He stared at the address, 1 Truth Road. Then he said,

"You know what. To hell with the Truth. It can wait. I'm gonna go find Jesus."

She laughed. The light made a diagonal cut through her face, and there was sadness in the angel and fury in the devil. She laughed in the middle.

"I *wouldn't* lie to you, Jim," she said. "Not because I wouldn't lie, but because the lie wouldn't work. You're a man who can't be lied to." She gave him a folded and tattered paper that was yellow with age.

He unfolded a map of *paradise*. It was marked with triangle trees and up-arrow mountains, poofy clouds and asterisk cities. There were also dotted-line highways and snaky rivers. And left of center there was scrawled an X with the caption, *Christ be here.*

X

1

Now Jim came to the place where the X was Jesus. It was a lake. He rented a canoe and rowed about on the *surface* of the lake, and he looked about on the *surface*, but he couldn't find Jesus. There were many trees and rocks and there was a great deal of sky, but there weren't any ripples in the water.

Then he came to where the lake became narrow. It twisted through roots and shallows and opened up into an austere cove. The water looked like a block of metal that reflected the sky. In the middle of it a small man fished from a wooden raft.

Jim paddled up to him. "Uh, Mr. Christ?"

The man didn't move. He sat upon the wooden raft with the wooden pole. He looked into the water.

"I'm sorry to bother you, Mr. Christ," Jim said. "I know you're retired. And I really don't believe in you. Or at you. On you. However that works. I came out here and I'm bothering you because there's a lot of people that *do* believe, and they're pretty mixed up about it. Like, they're blowing *paradise* to hell because of some things you said once. I've heard it was mostly nice things, and I don't really get it, but I thought maybe you could, I don't know, give them the business. Set them straight. Or something."

The man said, "I've been fishing this spot for three hundred years. Three hundred years, and I haven't caught a single fish."

"That sucks."

"If a man casts his pole into a pond that has no fish, does he deserve to eat?"

Jim thought, Man, not this shit again. He said, "I'll be completely honest with you, Mr. Christ. I don't care. Questions like that have been getting me shot out of cannons and sucked into black holes. I'm done with them. I mean, your followers are ripping *paradise* apart, and you're out here fishing."

"Josh."

"What?"

"My name."

"Well, alright Josh, I'm Jim."

"I'm glad to meet you, Jim. But the politics of *paradise* no longer interest me."

"The fuck they don't!" Then Jim realized he just yelled fuck at Jesus, who was Josh, and he pulled back a little. "I'm sorry. Maybe that wasn't called for. But you're the guy at the center of the whole thing. They're all fighting for different versions of *you*."

"No they aren't."

"Yes they are."

"Not really."

"Goddammit they are! Sorry."

Josh pulled up his wooden pole and the hook and the lure came out of the water. He opened his tackle box, changed the lure, and cast off again.

He said, "They'd rather die for the things they can't see, than live with the ones they can. One look at me and they'll say, Oh well that's not really *him*, and they'll go right on dying."

"That's the problem. Nobody's dying," Jim said. "And isn't that why *you* died?"

Josh laughed at this. It was a deep laugh that came from his gut. "You know, I tried doing it for a while," he said. "Playing the savior. There was this one time, I went to some Pope or another, just to talk. I don't remember why. And he believed who I was, or at least who I *had been*. And suddenly, in the middle of our conversation, he looked at me and said, Listen buddy, all I need to know is, are you a Catholic? When I said no, he had me thrown into a sack and they buried me under the Stupid Fucking Mountain. It took me a decade to crawl out."

"Hey," said Jim. "I climbed that mountain."

"Everyone climbs the Stupid Fucking Mountain."

"Well, I climbed it too."

"The point is, none of it has anything to do with me. So I'm done with it. And I told her that those firmaments were a bad idea, but she was desperate. I'm curious, what finally brought them down?"

"It's not important," Jim said. "They're down and nobody is special anymore and they're pissed off about it. I came here to get you to talk to them, but evidently it's hopeless."

They stared together at the place where the fishing line met the metal block of water. Jim expected the line to jerk at any moment, and for Josh to finally catch his fish. But though they stared for a long time, nothing broke the *surface*.

And Josh said, "What did you do in life?"

"What do you mean?" said Jim.

"What work did you do? How did you eat?"

"Well, I just worked, really. Welding was good money. I did some roofing and drywalling. Whatever I could find."

"We are not so different. I also just worked. Mending ploughs, building houses. I even did some roofing." Josh looked Jim in the eye for the first time. "Would you give another man the road because he had clean hands? Would you accept his whip when you didn't give it fast enough?"

"No," Jim said. "I'd shove that whip right up his ass."

"Well, we had hammers and empty stomachs, and the Romans had armor and feasts. They were chosen by many colorful gods and we were slaves to a dark one. So one day, after three Roman soldiers raped and killed a friend of mine, I stood on a crate and said, I am a son of God.

"Between the Aramaic of the people, and the Hebrew of the Scholars, and the Greek of Romans, the *a* became a *the*. Articles don't translate so well. I became *the* son of God, and a few years later the fuckers nailed me to a cross."

It was Jim's turn to laugh, a deep laugh that came from the gut.

"I can't help you," Josh said.

"Seriously though, you've got to give me something. I came a long way."

"Work."

"Huh?"

"You said you were a roofer. The firmament is a roof."

"There's a war in *paradise* because the devil lied, and now that the lie is broken the advice of Jesus Christ is that I *board it up*?"

"My name is Josh."

So Jim took his leave of the small man on the wooden raft. When he reached the edge of the cove, the man called out some parting words:

"Jim! Before you cast off, make sure there's fish!"

2

With a bag full of nails, a good hammer, and planks of wood donated by the Presbyterian Church of Canada, Jim went to work. He started where the crack in the firmament met the ground and he worked his way up. And though he doubted that the advice of Jesus who was Josh had been sincere, it felt good to hammer in the nails. It felt good to *work*.

And he worked for a long time. Days and then weeks and then years came to pass. He went through thousands of boards and millions of nails. He didn't eat and he didn't sleep. He didn't look up because it discouraged him, and he didn't look down because it frightened him. He looked at his hands and at the place where the hammer met the nail.

But then one day the hammer broke and Jim looked around. He was a mile high over the shredded fields of war. His labor trailed behind him as a wooden rainbow. Then he put his eyes forward and beheld that he had the whole sky to go.

"I don't think this is gonna work," he said.

Now a friendly and wise old face popped in through the crack in the firmament. "Jim!" it said. "You goddamn crazy hillbilly! You can't fix the sky with wood!"

"Einstein. Well, your dice didn't work for shit, either," Jim said.

Einstein pulled himself up and mounted the firmament like a horse. "I'll make it up to you," he said.

"Yeah?"

"This breach is distorting the *antiverse* as well. Since it occurred my findings have been entirely anomalous. But I think I've found a way to patch it."

"Alright."

"Do you remember what I said about philosophy, Jim? The thoughts that can't produce phenomena and the hyper-expansion of *paradise*? It turns out that all thought, phenomenally charged or not, travels through the vacuum at exactly the speed of light. I have observed in the antiverse for the first time the velocity of philosophy, and against all intuition the non-phenomenal traverses the plane at the same speed as the phenomenal. The difference is, the non-phenomenal – philosophy – is constantly changing direction, with such frequency and redundancy that it never gets to where it is going. All of this churning and digressing eventually feeds back on itself, and the resulting energy is proportional to the square of the value of the original asininity. And though each individual asininity is very small, the cumulative effect is what we observe as the hyper-expansion of the phenomenal sphere. I have discovered the Paradisial Constant!"

Jim scratched his head. "Didn't we go over this before?"

"And here is the homerun kicker." Einstein spurred the firmament with the heel of his boot. "The physical reason that philosophy cannot produce phenomena, is that non-phenomenal thoughts propagate entirely on waves. Without the particle-wave duality of phenomena, these philosophical waves cannot collapse. They can form nothing of substance."

Jim understood none of it. He said, "Is there any fish back there? Jesus said we should get some fish."

"What?"

"Nothing."

"Fish?"

"Yeah."

"Anyway, I've examined what's left of this firmament,
110

and I believe I understand its function. Religious philosophy, like all philosophy, is based on several core asininities. While these asininities cannot produce phenomena, the waves carry a certain frequency. It is usually undetectable, but within a particular religion the same asininity is produced by a billion minds and the signal is strong enough to detect. The firmament is fitted to receive these signals, identify the religion of origin, and then filter out whatever phenomena that religion opposes. It's simple and ingenious, and I may be able to improve upon it."

But it did not sound so simple to Jim. He said, "So what do you need me for?"

"I'm coming to that, hillbilly." Einstein pointed through the crack. "Some of these religious waves have seeped into my *antiverse*. Apparently, in the *antiverse* they can take form, and they're goddamn crazier than you are. I have succeeded in collecting them and I've gathered them into the gravity well of a dark star. After I infuse them with super particles and charm quarks I intend to ignite the quasar and point the energy beam directly at this breach. And that's where you come in."

"Of course it is."

"I need a distraction, Jim. I need you to distract every soul within the visual radius of the aberration. If a single pair of eyes looks up it will be a disaster."

"Well, wait a minute. That all sounds kind of awesome. Why can't we watch?"

And Einstein took Jim by the shirt and shook him. "Because! You goddamn crazy hillbilly. When your nut nuked a hole in the firmament you gave form to the madness of humankind! If it is observed before reentering the phenomenal sphere, the wave function will collapse and the heavens will be enslaved by the Immoveable Asininity!"

"Are you telling me God is back there?"

"Not God. The half-baked and ill-founded mutation dreamed up by the intellectually perverted. Now, take this walkie-talkie and contact me when the distraction is in play."

"You're fucking with me."

"Do you know the difference between science and religion, Jim?"

"Kind of."

"Results! Get me that distraction, and I'll get us a firmament."

3

So Jim sought out the one man he knew of that might supply such a distraction. He found the man in a cabin surrounded by autumnal woods. Jim explained to him that there was a crack in the firmament, and its mending required the stirring of the Christian fold.

"I won't do it," Hitler said.

"Oh come on."

"It's a bad idea."

Hitler sat upon a lawn chair on the deck of the cabin. The deck overlooked a creek that whispered through oak and pine. On the table beside the chair there *was* a paperback novel, and the Fuhrer sipped on a pineapple pina colada.

"I golf now," Hitler said. "I tell jokes. I read books. I no longer incite calamity."

"Just do it one more time. That's all I'm asking. Just one more."

"It's too reckless. You couldn't even get Jesus to do it."

"So you're gonna bitch out just cause that's what

Jesus did?"

"I am *not* a bitch." Hitler sipped on his pineapple pina colada. He looked out upon the autumnal woods. "Though I must admit, all of this relaxing can get very tiresome. Sometimes I wonder if a *little bit* of calamity might do me some good."

"That's what I'm talking about."

"So all I have to do is distract them? I don't have to holocaust anybody?"

"Nope. No holocaust."

"I don't know . . ."

"What's the problem?"

"I'm rusty. I wouldn't know what to say."

Jim made the guffaw. "Dude, you broke Europe. Like, a substantial number of the people that are up here, they're up here because of you. A hundred million, two hundred. I don't know exactly, but it's a lot. And I know you don't get any credit, but that was you, man. You did that."

Hitler nodded. He drank the last of his pina colada. He picked up the paperback and thumbed through its pages. "This *is* a terrible book," he said.

"So you'll do it?" Jim said.

Hitler stood and stretched his back and his legs. He said, "I will do it, but we must become homosexual partners."

"Uh, what?"

And Hitler put his hand on Jim's shoulder. "My lips are going to finish what your dick has started."

Jim got it.

4

Einstein. Einstein, come in. Are you there?

Jim! I am in orbit around the dark star. The apparatus is fully operational. Is the distraction in play?

It's ready, but it might take some time.

After detonation, it will take two minutes for the charm quarks to reach the firmament. Not a single person can witness it. No observers! Our timing must be perfect!

Do not detonate until I give the word. I repeat, Do not detonate.

What is the distraction? Fireworks? A John Wayne movie?

Uh, well, not exactly. Would that have worked?

Anything that draws the eye. We only need a picosecond. What is in play?

I went with Hitler.

What?! You goddamn crazy hillbilly!

5

So Hitler came to the field of battle. He stood upon the shoulders of a smirking angel who floated above the blasted ground. A microphone descended from the sky. Hitler tapped it with a finger and the thud echoed through the sound system of *paradise*. There was the *wang* of feedback and he cleared his throat.

He said, "What is the difference between a Jew and a hooker?"

Jim thought, That sonofabitch, if he starts holocausting people I'm not golfing with him anymore. He lay on a hill at the edge of the blasted ground, with binoculars in one hand and Einstein's walkie talkie in the other. And the voice of Hitler was clear through the sound system.

"The difference is, I have only instigated the murder of two hookers. Get it? I am the Fuhrer. The joke is funny because it is not really a joke and it is inappropriate for me to tell it. Don't worry, I have many more."

Throughout the blasted ground the heads began to *turn*. For though they loved the war, they *really* loved a spectacle. Muskets and shovels became leaning sticks and the Fuhrer had a small audience.

"How many Jews does it take to change the lightbulb?" Hitler said. "Anybody? The answer is zero. It is zero because Jews now live in a terrible darkness, for which I am partly responsible, and they have lost the will to change the bulb. This guy gets it."

Jim followed the finger of Hitler, and he saw through the binoculars the oscillations of a papal cap. Then he heard upon the wind the *hurrrr hurrrr hurrrr*.

And Hitler told many more jokes. The small audience became a *fashionable* one. There came the Anglicans and the Lutherans and several Orthodoxies, and there came the Methodists, the Baptists, the Mormons, the Evangelists, the Congregationalists and the Pentecostals. They wandered in with weapons low, and they were glad for the reprieve and they laughed together at the saviorless Jews.

Then the Presbyterians came. They brought enough cake for everyone. And when the Catholics came, the din of war was no more. Hitler now stood at the pinnacle of all attention, high on the shoulders of the smirking angel.

He said, "But I have not come before you today to tell jokes or do the holocaust. I am here to show you all my true colors. I am in my heart the artist who died in Vienna, and to prove it I am going to paint for you a masterpiece. I call it, The Prophet Mohammed Enjoys an Ice Cream Cone."

Then a second smirking angel brought to Hitler a

canvas and a pallet and a brush. Hitler dipped the brush in the pallet and began to paint the likeness of the Islam prophet upon the canvas.

"Oh *shit*," Jim said.

6

Einstein! Now! Fire! Fire!

What's happening down there?

Hitler is painting Mohammed! Eating an ice cream cone! I don't know much about Islam, but you don't fucking paint Mohammed. We gotta go now.

Dammit, hillbilly. Elvis, you could have called up Elvis. Alright, we have detonation. Two minutes to arrival.

Can you make it go faster?

Charm quarks do not have a gas pedal.

He's starting with an outline. He's outlining. Looks like a body. Those might be arms. There's a head taking shape.

One minute, forty seconds.

I can definitely make out the ice cream cone.

One minute, thirty seconds.

You know, he's pretty good. Like, he's really got a knack for this. It's kind of sad how good he is. I think this painting is really going to come together.

One minute remaining to impact. Is the distraction complete? A single observer, Jim! A single eye looking up and the charm quarks will collapse, and you will all be slaves to the Immovable Asininity!

Nobody's turning away from this shit. He's working on the eyes.

Forty seconds.

The eyes are brilliant. It's like, they're looking

through me, man.

Twenty seconds. Jim, if this works, there will be an immense burst of light followed by, well, followed by *something*. It will probably be disorienting.

I'll be damned. He finished. Mohammed is enjoying an ice cream cone. Oh shit. Einstein, there's another crack! The *jihad* is coming!

7

Ka-fuckin-*boom*.

8

Jim! Jim, come in! Was there a flash? Are you disoriented? Damn you, hillbilly, what's going on down there?

I, I'm here. Yeah, I'm still here.

Did it work?

I don't know. There was a huge burst of light. I don't see the crack in the firmament anywhere. Something's weird, though.

What is it? Can they see each other? They should not be able to see each other.

It's, like, the opposite.

The opposite?

We can see *everything*. Inside and outside. It's like we can look into each other's thoughts. It's hard to explain. But we can definitely see each other.

A million pole dancers in *paradise*, and you give Hitler a paint brush. Do you see anything that is either immovable or asinine? I will roast your hillbilly hide on a spit if we created a god.

No, it's nothing like that. I mean, it's *awesome*. We're all looking around right know and finding out that we pretty much think the same things. Like, we're all scared shitless when it comes to spiders and the darkness, and music is a good way to fill up your time, and there's something about a laughing baby that makes everybody feel warm inside. Even the stuff about the God and the unknown, we're all just sort of confused and hopeful about it. It sounds crazy, but it just got real friendly down here.

Results!

9

Then Jim found Lucy on a low-hanging cloud. She was *all* Lucy now, and there were bags under her eyes. Jim stood beside her in silence. Together they surveyed the peaceful throng of all religions.

And the throng *was* peaceful, but it was also stirring. For the memory of the spectacle, which they called the miracle, was quick to fade. They began to argue about the details of the miracle, and it looked like they might form new factions and go to war for the oneness of humankind.

And then it began to rain fish.

"Are you doing that?" Jim said.

"No," Lucy said.

Jim pulled out the walkie-talkie. "Einstein, it's raining fish."

The walkie-talkie cackled. "Is that some kind of hillbilly riddle?"

"No, it's raining fish. Does that have anything to do with the charm quarks?"

"Well, in theory, if enough super neutrinos from the *antiverse* run up against the charm quark barrier with sufficient simultaneity, any number of strange phenomena could be localized there. Fish rain is a bizarre, but possible, outcome."

And the fish fell and *fell*. Children played with the fish as swords. Some of the fish fell in water and were fished again. Disputes were settled by fish-throwing contests. Protestants and Catholics and Muslims made fish angels together. Then the *hipsters*, called Larry Goldstein and Gary Steinberg, began to collect and sell the fish. And there was also some fish *juggling*.

Then a single note from a faraway horn dangled in the rain. Jim knew the cadence, for it *was* a French horn, and a rainbow came through the sky.

And Lucy, who called herself the devil, who played herself an angel, watched the people and the fish. The bags beneath her eyes were the shadows *of* exasperation. Jim said to her,

"You know what Jesus said to me?"

But Lucy stopped him with her hand. "I don't care," she said. "I just need a drink."

XI

1

So Jim came to Small Town, Paradise. There were green yards and clean airs and split-level houses. There was a post office, a police station, a grocery store, five bars, and one set of well-kept stop lights. Autumn cooled the afternoons and summer warmed the evenings, and every evening there was a new episode of Financially Stable and Moderately Happy Family.

Jim walked down the street through the split-level houses. He came to a *particular* house, for it was painted white and there was a garden and a fence. Though the lawn was already clipped to quarter-inch perfection, a stoical man mowed *it*. He marched in rigid lines over the square of grass until the grass had all been marched upon.

Then the stoical man cut the engine of the mower, stored the mower in the garage, and entered the house. Jim waited five minutes and knocked on the door. The stoical man answered with beer in hand.

"I was wondering when you'd come around," the man said.

Jim said, "Yeah."

"You've been in some of the papers, you know."

"I didn't."

"Well, I guess you better come in."

Jim followed the man to the room with the television. The man sat in the dominant recliner, and Jim upon the angled couch. Each waited for the other to speak. It took a while.

"Your mother left me," the man said.

"That sucks."

"She's a princess now. A Disney princess. You believe that?"

"I do."

"Said I spend too much time mowing the lawn. One look at *paradise* and suddenly keeping the house isn't her thing anymore. She wanted more. They always want more."

"There's a lot to do in *paradise*."

The stoical man drank long from the sweating beer. "A man knows what he has and he makes it work. A man doesn't go off chasing what he knows he'll never catch. A man builds a house, pays the mortgage, and keeps his lawn. That's what a man does."

"You have a mortgage?"

"Why'd you come here?" the man said.

"I'm not really sure."

"I don't have any money."

"It isn't money."

"You in trouble with the law?"

"The law? Are you serious?"

"Well, someone has to take things seriously around here."

"I nuked a hole in the sky. With my dick. There was a war. Angels cried. I'm not worried about the law."

"Sounds like you ought to be."

The man's posture upon the recliner was upright. His arm lay flat against the armrest and the ankle of his right foot was stable upon his left knee. He *was* sublime in his authority. And Jim thought, He's the king of the room with the couch and the television.

"You mind if I grab a beer?" Jim said.

"Not till you tell me why you're here."

"I really don't know."

"Neither did your mother. You want a beer, you tell me what the fuck you're doing here."

Jim stood up instead. "You're not having any of it, are you? You're still back in Tennessee. Does Uncle Zeke live seven houses down? Is there a Thursday meat raffle you get racist drunk at? I bet you still wake up at five-thirty and polish those ugly boots."

"I served my country in those boots. I love those boots. They remind me that I did something once and I keep them clean. I also built the room you're standing in and I sowed the lawn you walked through to get here. And I know exactly why I did it. I did it because this is where I want to be and this is how I want to live."

"You're fucking dead!"

"You're only dead when you run out of reasons. I got mine, where's yours?"

Jim *had* no answer.

"That's what I thought." The stoical man finished off the beer. "You're my son, Jim. But your whole life you been flopping around like there's a hook through your lip. I don't know who put it there, but it sure as hell wasn't me. Now, Financially Stable and Moderately Happy Family is on in five minutes. So if you got nothing else to say to me, say something to the door."

2

Therefore Jim went to Disney Land. He came to a pavilion that was filled with color and children. Parents sat on benches and drank cold beverages, or they looked through the windows of the shops that gave away trinkets. In the garden there grew the flowers of imagination and its cobbled paths turned only for the heart.

The only *drab thing* was a woman in soot-stained rags. She stood in the center of the happiness. She handed out candies and kisses that she pulled from the air. Jim was careful not to step on any dreams when he walked up to her.

"Mom?"

"Jim!" She hugged him. "What a lovely surprise!"

"You look so young," he said.

"I *am* young." It was a playful warning. She spun, and her soot-stained rags spun *with* her. "I was always young. I'm so glad you finally came. That life, oh Jim, it wasn't me!"

"I guess not. You look really nice. I mean, even in the dress. It's a nice dress, too. I just mean, it's nice. Everything is nice."

"I'm Cinderella," she said. Then she touched his cheek. "And you look good, too. Why don't we take a little walk?"

There was some pouting when Jim stole the princess away. But when the princess told them that her glass slipper was hidden somewhere in the garden, and that the first to find it would ride the magic pumpkin, the transgression was forgotten.

They walked until they were alone.

"They really love you," Jim said.

"Oh, I love them, Jim! I love them so much! And I love this place. The colors, the magic, all the smiling little faces. It's *paradise.* It's really *paradise.*"

"I wish I could find something like this. You know, something that fits."

"There's always room for another Jack Sparrow."

"I don't think I'd be much of a pirate."

"I think you'd make wonderful pirate."

"Thanks, Mom."

"Oh! Stop! Over here! *Shhhhhh.* Here he comes."

And Cinderella pulled him to the side of the cobbled walk and into the shade of the bell flowers. A stiff man in a serious suit appeared upon the walk. He carried upon his shoulder an enormous paint brush, the way a soldier might carry a bazooka.

"That's Walt," she said. "Look, he's about to change something."

Walt considered what surrounded him and then he went to work with his brush. The blues and the reds and greens and the yellows swirled out of comprehension. A new *form* took shape. It was a little thatch hut with wayward dimensions and a smoking chimney. Then a family of penguins walked out of the hut. They wore Hawaiian shirts and started a barbecue.

"Jim . . ." Cinderella touched his elbow. "There's another reason I like it here."

"What?"

"I get to be close to your brother."

"I have a brother?" For Jim had never *known* a brother.

Cinderella pointed. Jim followed her finger over the thatch hut and the tress and a patch of giant mushrooms. The peaks of a castle glittered against the painted sky.

"In the tallest tower. That's where they go."

"They? How many brothers do I have?"

"It was a long time ago, Jim. Please forgive me, that I

never told you. How could I know? How can anybody know?"

"Mom. Mom, it's alright. Really. What's going on?"

"I didn't want him. I *couldn't* want him. It was so long ago, and in that dreadful *life*. Before I met your father, I . . . I let him go."

Then Jim understood. He took Cinderella's hand, for it was also his mother's, and he pressed it in both of his. "You had an abortion?" he said.

She nodded.

"And abortions go to the tallest tower in the Disney castle?"

"No one else would take them." Cinderella wiped a tear from her sooty cheek. "Before Walt, the unwanted were unwanted even here. But he changed all that. They have a home now. He's a wonderful man."

Walt, who was satisfied with the hut and the penguins, walked on down the cobbled path. He let the tip of the brush trail along the top of a hedge row, and many-colored birds and beetles sparkled out of its wake. Then Walt turned with his heart and the path turned with him and he was gone.

"Can we visit him? In the tower?" Jim said.

"You go." Cinderella smiled. "I owe a lucky little prince a magical pumpkin ride."

3

"Hi-ya Jim!"

"Hi. Mickey Mouse."

"So you're here to see your brother! That's just great!"

"Yeah."

"Don't look so glum, Jim! You're gonna love it! We

have the best facilities in *paradise*!"

"So I've heard."

"Well let's cut the chit chat and get on with it then!"

Jim followed Mickey to the rotunda. There were marble busts of Aladdin and Muriel and Snow White and Simba and Dumbo and R2D2 and Pocahontas and Cinderella. And high on the wall above the doors to the tower there was a mural. The mural showed a happy family tossing their baby into the clouds, and Goofy waited there with a baseball mitt.

"Why Goofy?" Jim said.

"He's the least visually abrasive!"

Mickey pulled a chain that hung from the dome and the doors to the tower came open. They walked into the tower. Jim beheld the collected abortions of humankind.

The fetuses floated in jars that climbed up the tower walls. Each jar was fitted with an iPad and headphones. The iPads dimmed and flashed in unison as the fetuses all streamed the same show. Jim tried to estimate the height of the tower and the number of fetuses, but the tower was too high and the number too great.

"How many are there?"

"Millions! And thousands more come every day!"

"And you just hook them up to iPads?"

"They were donated by Steve Jobs! Isn't he great?!"

"What are they watching?"

"What time is it?!"

"Four-thirty."

"They watch Fox News from four to five!"

"Fox News." This wasn't a question. It wasn't a statement either. It merely fell out of Jim's face.

126

Mickey said, "Well, it turns out you don't have to have thumbs or be conscious to have a political affiliation! And they're all conservative on account of being aborted!"

Jim thought, It kind of makes sense that the aborted fetuses in *paradise* would be pro-life conservatives. I mean, I doubt they really give a shit about the economics of it.

Mickey led him to a mine cart. They climbed in. Mickey handed Jim a hard hat and said, "Safety first!" And then he pulled a lever and the cart began to climb the tower on a winding track.

The cart carried them up and around and up. The jars with the fetuses were packed in ten deep. The fetuses had many shapes and sizes. Some of them were large and well-formed, and these looked like pig runts. Others were little more than strings of goop. Upon them all the iPads flashed in constant rhythm.

"Why can't they be people up here?" Jim said. "They're just a bunch of DNA, right? It seems like, since we're in *paradise* and we have all this technology, we ought to be able to grow them into people."

"It's a consciousness problem!" Mickey pumped an upbeat fist. "We tried growing a batch of em but nobody's home! They just walk around like zombies and mumble and drool! That's why we're looking for activities that don't require the spark of humanity!"

"So what can they do? Without consciousness?"

"Well, let's see. We already talked about politics. They can also browse the internet and post memes and clever comments! A few of them even have blogs and facebook pages! And they're just great at Candycrush!"

And the mine cart carried them up. Jim looked over its edge and saw that they had climbed about twenty stories. The top of the tower was still a point in the distance.

"I don't think I like where this is going."

"What's the matter, Jim?! Afraid of heights? Just think of down as up's best friend. That's what I always do!"

"I – wait, what? No. How much farther is it? And how do you know which one is my brother?"

"Steel trap!" Mickey knuckled his head. "And look at that, we're already here!"

The mine cart came to a stop. Mickey pulled out from the wall of jars a single jar. The fetus that floated within it was on the *cusp* between a pig runt and a string of goop. Mickey handed the jar to Jim.

"Does he have a name?"

"Nope!"

"How do we know he's a he?"

"Science!"

And Jim beheld the fetus of his brother. He tried to imagine where the arms and legs would have grown, and where the head would have taken shape. He imagined eyes full of wonder and a mat of messy hair.

"Can I take him away from this place? Like, if he had a home?"

"Sorry, Jim, but that's impossible! It's against company policy to let copyrighted material walk out the door!"

"Copyrighted?"

"Copyrighted!"

"Walt Disney copyrighted my mother's abortion." Neither a question nor a statement, it fell from Jim's face.

"He's an entrepreneur! But you can chat with your

brother any time you like!"

"I can talk to him?"

"Sure! Here's his Skype id!"

So Jim entered the Skype id of his aborted brother into his phone. He thought for a long time about what to say.

4

Jim

Hi

01101010 01101111 01100101

Wat

Jim

We've never met before, but I'm your little brother. We have the same mom. I'm Jim.

01101010 01101111 01100101

dafuq?

Jim

Yeah, I know it's pretty weird. But it's true. I just found out about you a few hours ago. Mom is a princess and my big brother is floating in a jar in the tallest tower of the Disney castle. I would have visited sooner but I didn't know you existed. We're brothers.

01101010 01101111 01100101

cool story bro

Jim

Do you like it here? In the tower? Is Mickey treating you alright?

01101010 01101111 01100101

I guess you could say they

(•_•)
(•_•)>⌐■-■
(⌐■_■)

fetus well

Jim

Oh, I get it. Feed us well. And it's like a well of fetuses. You know I'm not sure I believe Mickey about this consciousness thing. I would think if you can make a pun you can be a person.

01101010 01101111 01100101

fag

Jim

What?!

01101010 01101111 01100101

FAG

Jim

All I'm saying is if you want me to I'll punch Mickey in the nose and we can bust out of here and maybe get you some legs. Get Einstein or Jesus to take a look at you, see if anything can be done.

01101010 01101111 01100101

3edgy5me

Jim

What the hell does that even mean?

01101010 01101111 01100101

u don't even

Jim

Don't even what?

01101010 01101111 01100101

bro

Jim

Are you fucking with me? Are you alive? Are you conscious?

01101010 01101111 01100101

nice try, socrates

Jim

I'm just trying to help my brother out. Say something meaningful if you're in there.

01101010 01101111 01100101

hi every1 im dead!!!!! shivers in jar I dont have a name but you can call me t3h PuNt3d EmBuRRiTo!!!!! lol i mexicant eat food!! thats why i came here, 2 meat ppl like me . . . im a tiny ball of goo (twisted 4 prenatal tho!!) i like 2 watch chefwars cuz they make SOOOOOO much food_ u always want what you cant have lol!!! its my fav show =) i dont have many friends bcuz goos h8 food \o/ BOOOOO!!!!! Boos 4 t3h goos h8in food!! lol .. neways theres no scapin 4 me so plz dont give me false hopeses);

EmBuRRRRRRRRRiTo!!!!!!!!!!!!!!! <----- me gettin twisted o.O haha .. byebye

5

When Jim came out of the castle Cinderella was waiting for him. She was the magical Cinderella now and her pink marshmallow dress filled the pumpkin carriage. Jim climbed in and the white mares pulled them away.

"I thought you were entertaining a prince," Jim said.

"Oh Jim! He was such an adorable little thing! He demanded to know why Aladdin didn't just wish for happiness. He said, maybe Aladdin would get Jasmine, maybe not, but at least he'd be happy about it, and he wouldn't have to do all that dancing and singing. I tried to explain to him, that's just not how it works, that's not how any of it works, but he wouldn't have it. Absolutely adorable! Did you talk to your brother?"

Jim nodded. "Yeah. We had a, uh, conversation."

"Isn't he the sweetest thing you ever saw? I wish I could just eat him up!"

"He called me a fag."

She slapped his leg. "That's between brothers. I don't need to hear that sort of thing. So tell me everything. What did you two talk about?"

"I'm not sure. I really have no idea what just happened. I mean, you've talked to him before. Do you think there's a person in there?"

"He's your big brother. Isn't that enough?"

"No."

"It should be."

"It isn't."

"Well what do you know about it? You don't know. Nobody knows anything about anything. You're just like your father, always taking things so seriously. Except you're not really serious at all, are you? Oh I don't want to talk about your father, it makes me sad. We are not talking about him. Your brother, mommy's little angel, is beautiful and he's happy and Mickey Mouse is taking good care of him. And that's how it works. That's the way of the world."

Her anger was *sudden*. Jim waited for some moments to pass. Then he said,

"Mom, I'm sorry."

"He's happy, Jim."

"Yeah, of course he is."

So Jim looked out the window. The white mares

clopped down a path through some trees and came beside a pond. It was a lonely pond at twilight. It was the kind of pond where a wandering hero might see something new in his reflection. Jim wondered what he would see if he looked down into the water. He wondered if he would see happiness there, or the same old confusion.

"I love you, Mom," he said.

"I love you too, Jim. Don't be angry with me. I'd hate myself if you were angry with me."

"He misses you." Jim kept his eyes on the pond, for he could *not* look upon his mother. "He said he wishes you'd visit more often."

"Oh, did he really say that? I told you he was sweet. There was never a sweeter child, Jim, in all the world. He misses his mommy. My baby misses me." She squeezed his fingers with her hand. "Where would you like to go, Jim? I can give you a ride, but the magic only lasts until midnight."

6

Jim knocked at the door and the old man answered with beer in hand.

"Well?" the old man said.

And Jim stood with shoulders squared. "I'm here because I want to get drunk."

The old man considered him *thoroughly.* Then he opened the door for Jim to step inside. He said, "I guess that calls for the good stuff."

The backyard was cut to the same quarter-inch perfection and high rows of hedges made it private. There was a vegetable garden and a wood shed, a pit for fires and a rusty old charcoal grill. When the old man came out with a bottle of Irish whiskey and two tumblers, Jim was looking upon the weather.

"Does it ever rain here?" he said.

"On schedule." The old man sat down in the plastic chair next to Jim. He poured the Irish whiskey into the two tumblers. "Gonna be a thunder storm on the fifth. Sounds like a real blower. I suppose I'll have to get all of this into the garage. Might tape up the windows. I'll have to go down to Hank's for a tarp for the garden. That kind of rain, it just brutalizes your tomatoes. If you're around, I could always use an extra hand."

Jim took the offered tumbler. He tipped it in the old man's direction. "Thanks, Dad," he said.

They drank.

They didn't speak for a long time. It was a comfortable silence. The old man didn't have any questions and Jim didn't have any answers and they drank and they looked at the *quiet*. They were three tumbles into the night when Jim said,

"I guess you could be happy here."

"Happy?" The old man peered into his empty glass. "Happy isn't anything I would know about. Always sounded like a lot of bullshit to me. There isn't any suffering here, though, if that's what you mean. You don't get punched in the gut for no damn reason."

"Mom leaving wasn't a punch?"

"She had her reasons."

"Yeah, I guess she did."

"You went to see her?"

Jim nodded.

"That's good."

"I think she's happy."

"Well of course she is. She's in *paradise* for Chrissake."

They filled their tumblers and drank to *that*. And two tumbles later they were hashing out economics,

134

ethics, and a precise definition for fascism. They were less than a miracle away from solving all three in a single tumble, but a remark was made and they were forced to arm-wrestle until dawn. Jim passed out in the quarter-inch perfection, heavy under fading stars.

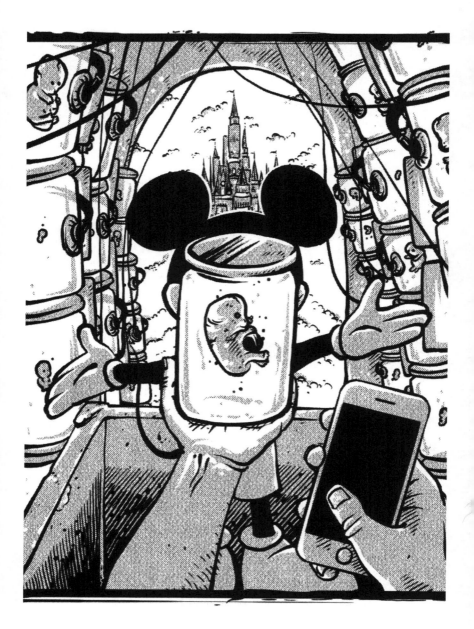

XII

1

"So. Jim. Why do you want to become an angel?"

"I think I'm pretty good with people," Jim said. "I've had to deal with various people types during my time here. Scientists, novelists, world leaders, philosophers, actors." He counted these *upon* his fingers. "If you look under recent job history there, I just helped the devil fix *paradise*. We had to bring a lot of different people together and get them motivated towards a unified goal. Like a, uh, *facilitator*. I *facilitated* a big project."

This was his first job interview in three hundred years. And, like Hitler, he was a little rusty. The executive woman who sat on the other side of the desk wore thin lips and thick glasses. She looked at him over the rims.

"A *facilitator*?" she said.

"Yeah. You know, a bringer-together. I brought all those people types together and we patched the hole in the firmament. Everyone went away happy."

"Do you even know what angels do, Jim?"

"Well, sure I do."

"What do angels do, Jim?"

The executive woman never blinked. In her office there was only the desk and a bookshelf. And the bookshelf had no books, for it was filled with potted cactuses. A clock without numbers ticked on the wall.

Jim cleared his throat. "They roll out the welcome mat," he said. "They keep the peace. Sometimes, anyway. When it suits them. The main thing about being an angel seems to be people. They're really good with people and they can bring people together. They're *facilitators*."

"That's it? They keep the peace? They *facilitate*?"

"Well, I've met a few that just seem to party and get high all the time. Heh."

But the executive woman was *not* amused. She removed her glasses and set them on the desk. She spoke with restraint through her teeth.

"Angels do not get high." She flipped through his file. "I've been screening applicants for a long time, Jim, and you're the worst I've ever seen. By far. You're reckless. You're aimless. Your libido is a tornado. The devil sought your *facilitation* because you set off a nuclear chain reaction in your girlfriend's *vagina* and started a religious war."

She used the word *vagina* like an axe. The blade hung in the air and over Jim's head. His body tensed and he waited for the blade to fall.

"And according to my records, after you nuked your girlfriend's *vagina* you just *left her there*. You haven't even called her back. Not even a text. Does that sort of behavior sound angelic to you?"

Jim gulped. "Cherry's cool," he said.

"The only reason I accepted to see you today was morbid curiosity. I asked myself, what sort of man spends the first three hundred years of eternity playing with his dick, and then applies to be an angel? What sort of ego? Does he really think he can walk into my office with nothing but a cock and a smile, and walk out with wings?"

Jim smiled. The executive woman slapped him through the face.

"Hey!"

"You're a pig."

"A pig in *paradise*."

She slapped him through the face.

"Dammit! Why are you hitting me?"

"Why are you here, Jim? Why have you come into my office and applied to be an angel?"

"I don't know. Maybe I'm just sick of wandering around. It would be nice to be useful, you know? I've never been useful. I never had a purpose before. When I was alive I wandered around and everything sucked, and now that I'm dead I wander around and everything is awesome – but I'm still just wandering around. Being an angel, I figure it's worth a shot. Maybe I can be shiny and useful, too."

These words surprised Jim as much as they surprised the executive woman. She leaned back in her chair and crossed her arms and beheld him. Jim beheld her back while he rubbed his cheek.

"Vulnerability suits you," she said.

So Jim said, "Thanks."

"But it doesn't wash away three hundred years of cocking around."

"Maybe not."

She walked to the bookshelf. After she sized Jim up, she chose from the shelf a cactus that was *six inches* tall and fairly thick. It wobbled when she set it upon the desk.

"Do you know what fascinates me about the cactus?" she said.

Jim shook his head.

"It's strong. It's resilient. It will quietly endure almost any environment, and stand resolute in the face of every adversity. I haven't fed this one in months and still it survives." She pricked her finger on one of its needles and showed Jim the blood. "And of course, it won't be tamed. Resilient, violent, and useless."

Then she took up a pair of scissors from her desk drawer. With the scissors she cut the cactus in half. Jim gulped again.

"Useless until you break it," she said. "Only then do you discover its utility." She lifted the cactus nub over her tongue, and from the nub there dribbled a pulpy white goo. The pulpy white goo dribbled into her mouth. It also dribbled down her chin. What dribbled down her chin she pushed back into her mouth, and then she swallowed.

Jim said, "I, uh, I want to be useful. But that's not how mine works."

The executive woman took out a pencil and some paper from the desk drawer. She wrote something on the paper and gave the paper to Jim.

"Before you take the entrance exam to become an angel, you'll have to take a course on modern women issues. Go to that address. They'll set you up."

And upon the paper was written, Nil Cunt Court – Sylvia Plath's Bottomless Pit of Feminist Revenge.

2

At the end of a middle class cul-de-sac Jim found a hole in the ground. It was large enough to swallow a house, and when he peered over the edge he couldn't see the bottom. He plugged his nose and jumped in.

He fell for a long time. Then he fell for a while longer. The circle of middle class light shrank above the gravity of the hole until darkness came. He splashed down into something warm and sticky.

And it *was* a pool. The pool was surrounded by high

walls and lit by torches. The liquid had the texture of mucus and the smell of warm metal. Jim treaded.

"Why have you disturbed the sacred pool?" It was a woman's voice, soft but amplified by the acoustics of the cavern. Jim beheld a pale woman standing upon the wall.

"I'm here to take the modern woman course," he said.

"For what reason?"

"I applied to be an angel. They said I had to come here first."

"What do you know of the modern woman?"

"She's new?"

"Lesson one: The modern woman of *paradise* does not bleed. Her menstrual cycle is tuned to a secret frequency, transmitted over radio waves, and the fluids are collected in this pool."

Now Jim saw the outlet valves upon the walls. They spurted out more of the viscous fluid at irregular intervals. He thought, I got some in my mouth.

"There is only one way up," the pale woman said. She lifted her skirt and her bush rolled down the side of the wall like a banner. It was a bush of *centuries.*

Jim swam over to it, grabbed a fistful of the gnarled hair, pulled himself out of the menstrual goop. His hands were slick with the blood-mucus and the bush was unwashed and greasy. Lint and crumbs and flakes fell from the bush, to pepper the pool below.

In my mouth, he thought again.

When at last he pulled himself over the top of the wall, he was sticky with menstrual blood and fuzzy with the pale woman's bush lint. He *was* tarred and feathered.

He said, "Do all angles get their wings this way?"

"Some," the pale woman said. She jerked her leg and the bush rolled back up between her legs. She took down a torch from the wall. "Follow me."

3

The tunnels were dark and labyrinthine. The only light came from the pale woman's torch.

"Are you Sylvia Plath?" Jim said.

"No," the pale woman said.

"Where are we going?"

"You will see."

"Will there be a shower?"

"Perhaps."

They turned and turned again. Some turns they didn't take. They went lower and lower. Jim was uncomfortable in the sticky silence, but he could summon no cues to conversation. Then, after many turns, he said,

"So, what's with the zero? In the address. *Nil Cunt Court*, it's a funny address. I'd have thought you'd be on something like, Women Are Awesome Avenue. But you're at the court of zero cunts. It's a little weird."

"We are *nil* because all other numbers are either phallic or lesbian," the pale woman said. She walked like a ghost and spoke sharply. "Zero is a woman's only refuge from the chauvinist math of men."

Jim pictured the numbers in his head: 1234567890. The one was a *forthright* phallus, and so was the seven. But the others were mysterious to him.

"Is the two phallic or lesbian?"

"The two is an inverted ballsack and phallus," she said.

"Huh. And three?"

"Just balls."

"Four?"

"Three phalluses."

"A four is three dicks?"

"Yes."

"What's five?"

"Regular ballsack and phallus."

Jim mulled it over. The pale woman walked.

"So eight's the lesbian," he said. "What about six and nine?"

"You know very well what six and nine are doing."

"Well, there you go. That's mutual. They're both having fun."

"Please. Six is obviously the woman, and nine the man. Six is worth less and is upturned and submissive. She is a gagged bitch hanging from her ankles and she is ever at the mercy of the rapist nine."

And as the pale woman led him deeper into the feminist cavern, Jim quietly exercised his brain with the strange new arithmetic. He thought, A hard dick plus a pussy *is* a hard dick, but a hard dick *times* a pussy is a *pussy*. And a hard dick squared is itself. But two hard dicks added together is an inverted ballsack and limp dick, which if squared becomes three dicks. And three dicks squared is one hard dick and a gagged bitch.

"Huh," he said. "The square root of a rapist is balls."

"And every vagina increases a number's value by an order of magnitude," the pale woman said. "At least men got that much right."

Jim thought, If that's true for pussies it's probably

true for balls and lesbians and rapists too. And magnitudes come in multiples of hard-dick-and-pussy, together. He kept his reservations to himself and said,

"I had no idea that feminists had to learn math all over again."

Then they came to a round door. The pale woman opened it and Jim went through.

4

These are the courses that Jim took in the caverns of the Bottomless Pit of Feminist Revenge: Entrenched Symbolism as a Justified Means of the Objectification of All Women Everywhere, The Importance of Being Sensitive but not *too* Sensitive because that's Patronizing you Entitled Sonofabitch, Emotional Awareness and Dating the Empowered Woman, Pillow Talk 101, and Pillow Talk 201. He tested out of Feminist Mathematics.

And the final course was Natural Beauty and the Institutional Shaming of the Female Form. It was taught by a horrible fat woman who drooled and was also ugly. Jim sat at a kindergarten desk and looked at her with bloodshot eyes.

Now the horrible fat woman held up two pictures. In one picture there was a hot chick, and in the other there was a fat chick. And the horrible fat woman said, "Which of these do you prefer?"

"The hot chick," Jim said.

The horrible fat woman *whapped* his knuckles with a phallus. It *was* a ruler, but according to the Entrenched Symbolism course book it was also a phallus. The horrible fat woman said, "The correct answer is, I do not have enough information."

So Jim pointed to the picture of the fat chick. "That's a lot of information."

Whap!

"Beauty is a totality," she said. "And that totality has been fragmented by the misogynist media, hyper-sexualized at the expense of the Natural Woman, packed up and airbrushed for the gratification of Abusive Men. Did you even read the chapter on the commercialization of the female form? Open your book to page six hundred and seventy-two. No, seventy-*two*. Read the first sentence. Aloud."

Jim rubbed his knuckles. Then he rubbed his bloodshot eyes. And then he rubbed his temples. He read,

"The commercialization of the female form has normative blowback, and your male brain has been artificially rewired to appreciate only the immediate and physical aspects of a much deeper feminine glory."

"And do you suppose, by *deeper feminine glory*, the text refers to *hotness* or *fatness*?"

"No."

"Well then what do you suppose it refers to?"

"I don't know." Jim searched his brain. "Sense of humor. Intelligence. Abilities. It's saying I should pretend fat girls aren't fat because they might be cool."

"No, no, *no!*" The horrible fat woman *whapped* his knuckles with the phallus. "You search *beyond* the physical. Find the woman *inside*. It is your duty as a modern man to unlearn these perversions of sexual selection, and to accept and admire the Natural Woman."

But Jim *had* no more patience. For though he swam through the sacred pool of menstrual blood, climbed the bush of *centuries*, learned phallic algebra, and let a woman pay for his steak, he could *not* endure the Female Form. He squeezed out of the kindergarten desk and stood to surrender.

"You know what, I give up," he said. "I've got nothing against anybody, but I like what I like. And I like the hot chick. Because she's hot. If the price of being an angel is that I've got to like what I don't like, just count me out. I mean, what's wrong with sexual selection? And why the hell is she fat in *paradise*? I don't care. Keep the wings. And for the love of humanity show me the way out of here."

To Jim's surprise the horrible fat woman sighed with relief. She dug a finger into her scalp and unzipped herself from forehead to crotch. The fat fell to the floor. Out of it stepped an attractive young woman who was angry and sweaty. She was *even* the hot chick from the photograph.

"Seventeen hours?" she said. "Really? Seventeen fucking hours?" She went to a closet and took up her purse, and from the purse she took out a pocket mirror. "Ughh. I look like a truck stop whore."

"What's happening?" Jim said.

"The last room is a test," she said. "It's a test to see how long you can put up with our bullshit."

"Did I pass?"

"*Pass*?" She stuffed the fat suit into the closet. "*Did I pass*?" She stripped out of her unitard and was naked. She squatted to scour the purse. "One hour. You only have to last for one hour. Uhghhh! I can never find anything in here!"

"Well, why didn't you tell me?"

"I can't tell you. I lose my job if I tell you." She found some underwear and snapped it on. She pulled her hair back in a scrunchie. "I pick up one afternoon shift, and I get the wonderboy who shatters the fucking record. That bitch Susie owes me big time."

"So I passed."

"You fucking passed."

The hot chick pulled from her purse a short skirt, a tank top, a bracelet of beads, and a pair of high heels. Then she was dressed and out the door.

"Wait!" Jim followed her. "Is it over? Are you Sylvia Plath? Am I gonna get my angel wings?"

"I'm taking you to Sylvia, wonderboy." She applied make-up as she marched down the cavern in heels. "Seventeen hours. I ran out of shit to say, like, ten hours ago. What the fuck is wrong with you?"

Jim had to walk fast to keep up. "I thought you were fat," he said.

5

So Jim came to the apartments of Sylvia Plath. They were so deep in the feminist cavern that the gravity of *paradise* shifted, and everything was upside down. Sylvia sat in a cushioned chair upon the ceiling. She pursed her lips as she worked at a crossword puzzle. Jim clung to the floor and looked down at her.

"You're so deep you're upside down," he said.

Sylvia started to laugh, then plugged her mouth with a fist, and then she laughed anyway. She stood and walked over to Jim. They stood up-face to down-face.

"Jim," she said.

"Sylvia."

"I heard you gave poor Ashley quite the show."

"Ashley? Was that the, uh, the girl in the suit? Natural Beauty?"

"Seventeen hours. You doubled the record, you know."

"Doubled?"

"Doubled."

"Sorry."

"Most men, they just sit there, stiff as a brick, and take the punishment for as long as they can. They *endure*. But you, I think you tried to understand it."

"I guess I did. I had my doubts, though."

"Doubts. And what makes a man like Jim have doubts?"

"Well, when I added two rapists together, I got a hard dick and a lesbian. That was kind of hard to swallow."

Sylvia laughed again. She put a soft hand on his chest. She said, "You're a sweet man, Jim. A sweet man with a good heart." Then her smile *was* a razor, and she whispered into his ear, "I hope it's not a secret, because it isn't safe with me."

She kissed him upon the cheek. The kiss cut through his skin and entered a vein, and through the vein it found his heart and then his head. It died there, but its warmth lingered in his face.

"Do you have the paper?" she said. "I believe I have to sign something. And you can go get your wings."

Jim gave her the form. She signed it upon his forehead and folded it neatly and tucked it into his shirt pocket.

"And *did* you understand any of it?" she said.

"No," Jim said. "Not really."

"Would you believe we prefer it that way?"

"Yes."

Sylvia made the smile that *was* a razor, and she showed him the way out of the Bottomless Pit of Feminist Revenge.

6

The executive woman stared in amazement at the

form that made official the non-misogyny of Jim. Her thin lips wrestled her pointed nose and her eyebrows were raised high over the rims of her glasses.

"That's Sylvia's signature," she said. "I'd have bet the left side of *paradise* against it, but there it is in black and white. Jim is *not* a cock-around. I don't know how you managed it, but you did. I suppose I owe you an apology and some congratulations."

Jim said, "Don't mention it."

She filed the form away, and then she gave Jim the business eye. She said, "Unfortunately, your application did not survive the preliminary screening. It's already been denied."

Jim came near to *shitting*. "What?! How can that happen? I passed. I jumped through every damn hoop you threw at me. Who denied me?"

"There is a committee. They found you wanting."

"Why?"

"You're not pretty enough."

"Not pretty enough? What the hell is that supposed to mean?"

"Angels are pretty. You are not. Therefore your application has been denied."

"But – but that's institutional. The shaming of the form. You're objectifying me. Symbolism and heteronormativity. Emotions. What about my goddamn emotions?" Jim sputtered the jargon of the modern woman for *several* minutes. Then he gave the executive his alpha finger. He said, "You threw me into the lake of pussy fire! I watched The Notebook *twice*!"

But the executive woman was unmoved. "The gains of feminism do not apply to you."

"Well why the hell not?"

"It's swinging between your legs, cowboy." She looked at the numberless clock that ticked upon the wall. She shuffled a stack of papers. "Now, I suggest you take it like a man and remove yourself from my office, or I'll be forced to file a harassment charge."

As he left Jim swiped a cactus from the bookshelf. It was a foot tall and as thick as a soda can. "This is mine," he said.

"Take it. They grow like weeds." And the executive woman waved him away with the back of her hand.

XIII

1

It came to pass that Jim stood at 1 Truth Road. He was sad to leave *paradise*, but he knew in his heart-brain-balls that he was *not for* eternity. He thought, I suck at orgies and I'm too dumb for suffering, I started a religious war with my dick, my aborted brother called me a fag and I'm not pretty enough to be an angel. *Paradise* just ain't for me.

Cherry stood with him.

"It's funny how small it is," she said. "I figured it would be big, like a skyscraper or something."

"Yeah," Jim said. For the building *was* small. Then he took her hand and became sincere. "Cherry, I'm glad you came. You didn't have to. And I know you think I'm being an idiot."

"I really can't talk you out of it?"

"I don't think so."

"What do you suppose is in there?"

"I don't know. Maybe it's pie."

Cherry squeezed his hand. Jim returned the squeeze. It felt nice to touch another soul while standing before the Truth.

"I'm sorry I nuked your pussy and abandoned you in the fallout," he said.

"Oh, we don't have to talk about that." Cherry leaned her head on his shoulder. "This is the end for you. Let's just be together and share a moment before you go."

"Okay."

So they shared a moment.

"Are you sure it's okay?"

"My pussy?"

"Everything."

"Yeah, everything's okay. I like this place, Jim. I like waking up and not knowing what's going to happen. And I don't need to understand it."

"You think I'm being an idiot."

"I think it won't be enough."

"It's the Truth."

"The Truth is just another place to be. And when you get there, you don't ever get to go anywhere else. And it looks fucking boring."

Jim laughed. It *was* the laughter of the soul, for it started in his balls and rattled his heart and brain. And when the laughter was finished his kissed Cherry on the lips. He said,

"If you see the devil, tell her thanks. For everything."

"I will."

And Jim walked into the small building at 1 Truth Road.

2

The room was white. Behind a desk sat the bald bespectacled man, who *was* kind.

"You seek the Truth?" he said.

"I do," Jim said. "And you're the guy that tried to hook me up with the cancer virgin. You summonsed me to existential court. You do the Truth?"

"I do the Truth." The bald bespectacled man took out a folder from a cabinet. "And if you don't mind, there's a series of questions I'd like to ask you. This part is completely optional, but your honest answers help us improve *paradise*."

Jim shrugged. "Yeah, go ahead."

The bald bespectacled man took a fresh form from the folder and he made ready his pencil. Then he began with his questions.

"How awesome was our staff? These are all one to ten, by the way."

Jim thought of the angel who had given him pizza, and the angel who had gotten him high. He thought of the nice woman at the Mortality Plaza.

"Ten," he said.

"And how awesome was the company?"

Jim thought of Shakespeare and Einstein and Hemingway and Plato. He thought of Jesus, Marco Polo, Hitler and the devil. He thought of Cherry.

"Ten," he said.

"How awesome was the weather?"

"Ten."

"How awesome was the transportation?"

"Ten."

"How awesome was the architecture?"

"Ten."

"How awesome was the wi-fi?"

"Ten."

"How awesome was the plumbing?"

"Really?" For Jim could answer *ten* no more. "What does the plumbing have to do with it? Aren't there any questions in there about, I don't know, happiness? Peace of mind? Solidarity?"

"No, there aren't." The bald bespectacled man

smiled, and it *was* a kind smile. "I'm afraid all of that is none of our business."

"Well then what is your business?"

"Plumbing."

"*Plumbing.*"

"Plumbing."

"You know what, just mark me down for ten, the whole way. The plumbing, the wiring, the upholstery. Ten ten *ten.*"

"Fair enough." The bald bespectacled man nodded a *knowing* nod. It took him a long time to fill in all of the tens. Then he said, "Alright, there's just one final question and the survey is complete. Then we can get you settled up with the Truth."

"Shoot."

"If everything is a ten, why leave?"

"I have no idea. That's why I came here. To find out. Maybe I need a few sevens."

The bald bespectacled man made a note of it. He filed the survey into the cabinet. Then he pointed. "Just go down that hall, and you're looking for the second door on the right. Good luck."

3

It was a long walk through whiteness. Jim came to the second door on the right. He entered another white room, and behind another desk there was another bald and bespectacled man. Then Jim blinked, for it was *the* bald bespectacled man.

"Take a seat."

"You're the same guy," Jim said.

"I run things around here. Go ahead, sit down."

Jim sat. He looked at the man. He *gulped.* He thought, This man *is* kind. And I've seen him around a lot. He showed me to the virgin and bounced at the devil's party.

"Are you . . ." But Jim couldn't finish the question.

"Am I?" He *was* kind.

"Are you God?"

The bald bespectacled man clasped his hands upon the desk and leaned slightly forward. The white light played in his kind eyes. He said,

"My name is Leonard, and I'm from Arizona. I died of a gastrointestinal disorder in nineteen fifty-eight."

"Oh."

"I have two boys and a beautiful wife. I don't get to see them as often as I'd like, but I enjoy working. So far I've been fortunate enough to experience ninety different forms of employment. My goal is to someday break a thousand. My wife thinks I'm crazy. I ought to retire, you know."

"She sounds nice."

"I am not God."

"Yeah, I get it."

"Are you sure that you're ready for the Truth?"

Jim took a breath. He cracked his knuckles. He took another breath. "Alright. Yes sir. I'm ready. Hit me with it."

"Because once you know the Truth, there's no going back."

"I know."

"And you understand that you're doing this of your own free will. You aren't compelled in any way by an outside party."

"Well, I can only assume that. But yeah."

"And you understand that billions of souls are

perfectly happy to be happy without the Truth."

"Yes. Come on, you're killing me."

The bald bespectacled man unclasped his hands and relaxed his posture. He beheld Jim and said,

"Here is the Truth: For the last three hundred and seventy-six years, you have been existing in *paradise*, and *paradise* is kind of awesome."

And this was *all* he said. He said it as if it was *all* that needed saying. Jim waited for more words to come, but the bald bespectacled man had finished.

"That's not enough," Jim said.

"I'm afraid it never is." The man nodded his *knowing* nod.

"It's not even a catch."

"Of course it's not. It's the Truth."

"What about God? The Devil? Heaven and Hell and right versus wrong? Who runs this place? Where is it? What am I doing here?"

"Well, God is God, the Devil is the Devil, and I suppose morality is somewhere in between. You run this place because it's your *paradise*, and you're in *paradise* because you're dead."

"So God exists?"

"That really depends on how you look at it."

"Then what's the right way to look at it?"

"There isn't one."

"Well why not?!"

The bald bespectacled man spread wide the palms of his hands. His face *remained* kind, but it was also brutally sincere. "These aren't meaningful questions, and I can't help you," he said.

Jim became speechless. For those were his

questions, and the kind man said they were meaningless. He thought, The catch is that there is no catch. The Truth is that there is no Truth. It's fucking pie.

"The exit is through that door," the bald bespectacled man said.

It was a plain door.

"What's on the other side?"

"I have no idea."

"What?!! This is 1 Truth Road! I'll give you the rest of it, but that's a door. I'll be goddamned if you don't know what's on the other side of a door."

"I never went through it."

"Then you don't really know the Truth."

"I told you the Truth."

"What about the door?"

"That's where you leave."

"What's behind it?"

"I don't have a clue."

"Jesus Christ!"

"Still fishing."

Jim went to the door and he threw it open. But before leaving *paradise*, he looked back one last time.

"At least give me this. What's the point of this place? 1 Truth Road? It sure as hell ain't the Truth."

The bald bespectacled man stood. He walked to where Jim *was* and he put a kind hand upon Jim's shoulder. "This just wouldn't be *paradise* with you moping around," he said.

Jim went through the door.

Made in the USA
Lexington, KY
14 November 2015